Heir
to the
Ice Flame

Rose Harvey

BookReality
Helping Writers Become Independent Authors

To my parents,
Joy and Jeff,
for their love and support of my writing journey
over the years.

I was once a princess.

Someone respected, loved, and most of all, protected. In those times, I felt locked in and I hated it. Like the caged birds in our aviary, I longed to spread my wings and fly.

So I made a wish.

A wish which changed my world forever.

If only I could have known the results of that fateful night. I forgot to exercise vigilance and wisdom, like every princess should; like I had been brought up to do.

But, most of all, I forgot the saying 'be careful what you wish for'. This in itself, was my biggest mistake.

Chapter One

There were three rules by which I lived.

One: keep your head down so you don't interfere in other people's business.

Two: never stay in the same town for more than three months.

Three: always, *always* keep your hair covered.

One may think them strange, yet for me, they were essential, a vital necessity. And after living by them for ten odd years, they had become a habit.

The dream was the same nearly every night. Once again I saw Lyn's piercing face, white and terrified in the candlelight, as she thrust a dark hooded cloak into my arms. It was too large for me and I struggled to pull it over my shoulders as the fabric fell in heavy folds to the floor. But Lyn gave me no time to complain, she was already pulling on my arm, heading in the direction of the stables where she lifted me onto a horse. I was about to tell her that I couldn't possibly ride bareback when she cut off my thoughts by crying,

'Go, Milady Nina. Go!' With one fluid motion, she hit the horse's rump and it set off into the whistling night air. After a moment I thought I heard her call something out, and turned just in time to see her fall jerkily to the ground, an arrow protruding from her back.

I smothered a scream and turned back, urging the horse to plunge onwards through the darkness. I barely noticed as we fled the palace grounds or as the city streets flew past, the sound of hooves hitting the cobbles repeatedly swirled through my mind. It was deathly silent, almost as if every house had been cast under a spell and I couldn't help but feel a twinge of fear. It took all of my concentration to cling to the horse's body with my knees, hands clutching and twisted in the mane. After a while my body was screaming out in protest, muscles straining with tension, and yet all I could see was the image of Lyn's face imprinted on the back of my eyelids.

My eyes opened as abruptly as the vision had arrived. I took in one long shuddering breath and exhaled, fingers pressing lightly against my temples as I fought away the rush of faint nausea that greeted me every time I awoke. I always felt like this after one of those dreams; and in the past few months those same dreams had visited often, too often for my liking.

As soon as my stomach had stopped churning, I rose and dressed quickly, winding my long plait of hair into a low bun. When that small ritual was complete, I pulled out my mortar and pestle and a handful of cranberries from my pack. I crushed them into a fine pulp, grinding continuously until the skin was almost ground to nothing and the juice was all that remained. After pouring some of the juice onto my hands, I began the second part of my ritual, this time in front of a plate of polished copper. There was only one spot on my head that I focussed on: a long streak of white amongst the flaming red of my hair. Slowly but surely the white became tinged with red as I massaged it in with my fingers, so that it almost blended in with the rest of my hair. It wouldn't be noticeable from a distance, but close up there was an obvious difference.

For this reason, I always kept my hair covered under a plain brown scarf. If people knew about the streak of white then I would become exactly what I had been trying to avoid for so long: hunted.

There was a rapid knock on the door to my room, and in a sudden haste I thrust the remnants of the cranberries into my mouth and swallowed, before hiding the mortar and pestle in my pack. Within moments the door opened and Mrs Jenkins, my landlady and current employer, peered in to check that I was coming down to work.

'Karliah, you'd better hurry it up, you worthless girl,' she snapped, 'there's customers waitin' to be fed and tankards to be filled. I can't run an inn by myself. Get downstairs and get to work.'

She turned and left abruptly and I followed, already dreading the hours ahead. As the rush hour started and hungry people came in after a hard day's work, my landlady became stressed and unbearable and would take it out on me. As I entered the bar, I was assaulted by the vile smell of beer and body odour, which made my stomach churn even more. Several men leered at me as I went behind the bar, and began filling tankards with a steady hand, ignoring them. The last thing I wanted was for a drunkard to try to get too close to me, and luckily Keely would throw them out if they did.

Keely was the only decent hired guard in the township of Little Fleming. I thanked my lucky stars every day that Mrs Jenkins had employed him. He often melted into the doorway, disappearing almost completely from view until such a time came that he was needed. At once he would appear as if from the air itself and wrap a large burly arm around the offending drunkard and toss them out of the inn into the dark street. I was in awe of him, and was constantly amazed that he could look so sinister, with his long dark hair, hooded brows and bulging muscles. He looked almost exactly like one of the evil henchmen that Lyn had described to me as a child in bedtime fairy tales. However, this evil henchman had a soft spot. If a kitten or puppy had been left out to die then Keely would be the first to nurse it back to health. Many a time, when the last customer had left, Keely would bring in one of his new charges: a lizard, cat or a bird with a broken wing. It was through his constant care of animals that he found Lisette.

At first I had stared, astonished and amused, as Keely brought in the small budgerigar, laying it down carefully by the fireplace. Winter had just set in, bringing freezing gales and late night frosts that lasted until mid-morning. I'd just arrived in Little Fleming, and I watched cautiously from the shadows as Keely knelt down by the hearth. The poor creature was bedraggled and almost dead from cold, but Keely tended to it, his large chunky fingers stroking the feathers and gently restoring it to life. Within two weeks, Lisette had gone from an almost death-like trance, to fluttering around the rooms, before landing on Keely's shoulder and preening her green and yellow feathers proudly. It was Lisette who chose her name, for, by the second week, she had opened her beak and spoken it loud and true. Keely had been over the moon, and proclaimed to anyone that would listen that if Lisette could tell us her name then she was a very clever budgerigar indeed. Personally, I wasn't sure about the size of her brain because after that rare occurrence, Lisette had done absolutely nothing special. It was quite disappointing really.

When winter had ended I knew that Keely was waiting for Lisette to leave, as all of his animal charges had done eventually. Strangely enough, she didn't, preferring instead to remain sitting on his shoulder, staring down every customer with a beady eye. He had taken this in his stride, but on rare occasions a contented smile would spread across his face when Lisette perched on his shoulder.

The door opened, bringing with it a rush of cold air, jolting my mind back to the tankard I was filling. I hastily pulled it away before the beer overflowed and placed it in front of one of the newcomers. He didn't take any notice of me, but just leaned closer to his companions, whispering intently. They had formed a small group, clustering around the main speaker, whose dark eyes glanced frequently around as if to check that they were not being overheard.

Despite myself, I was curious. I leaned towards them while I filled the next tankard, feigning nonchalance. Deep inside I was burning to know what they were talking about, and thankfully, I could hear the man's low voice, which throbbed with strange passion.

'She's alive, I tell you. The Usurper has sent out ten more battalions in pursuit of her, he knows that she might hear of the Resistance, and seek to join them. He *knows* that she could be the only one to take back the throne.'

'But the princess has been missing since the Dark Time,' another interrupted, 'she's most probably dead, long dead.'

'Then why hasn't the Usurper declared it loud and clear, for the whole world to know?' The first man asked, 'surely news like that would diminish any hopes of retaking the land. The princess is the last remaining member of the royal family, the last hope for the People. If she died then the Usurper would trumpet his success, not keep it hidden.'

I had stopped breathing, frozen in shocked silence. Frantically I placed two more tankards in front of the group, hoping desperately that they would not notice me. I hadn't heard talk of any sort of Resistance for years, not since the last of the Usurper's Trackers had hunted them down in their mountain fortress and annihilated them. There were tales that smoke still emerged from the crumbling ruins of the last Resistance Stronghold, but no one dared go there. Would the Resistance really set themselves up again in the ruins of their last defence? Surely they wouldn't be that stupid, especially when the Usurper knew where the fortress ruins were. Or had the Resistance moved to a new, safer location? If so, where was it?

'Karliah, idiotic girl, what are you doing?' Mrs Jenkins snapped, as I realised that the tankard I was filling was overflowing. A pool of beer was forming around my feet, but I had barely noticed the damp entering my shoes. In a haze, I gave the final member of the group his beer and bent to mop up the spillage. On hearing my landlady's voice, the group had fallen silent and watched me shrewdly. I felt like cursing my employer, and myself for losing track of what I was doing, but hearing about the Resistance brought new hope. It meant that I had a place to go. A place to hide.

It was common knowledge in Scardia that I had escaped that night. The night had been the first of the Dark Time, which had lasted several years, casting a shadow of fear into the hearts of even the bravest men. I had been seven at that time; young, naïve and spoiled. When the Dark Time began my world was turned upside down, and for the first time in my life, I had to take care of myself. There weren't any servants or nurses, no mother or father to run to in times of trouble. And now - ten years later - I was almost eighteen, and eligible to ascend the throne as the laws of Scardia decreed.

The revival of the Resistance was probably no matter of luck. Its leaders must have remained vigilant, awaiting the year when I would turn eighteen, when I would be of use to them and their plans. I bit my tongue absentmindedly, lost in thought. What benefit could I really be to the Resistance? I had fled the palace before I could learn anything necessary about ruling the kingdom. My father died before my thirteenth year, the traditional moment when an heir to the Ice Throne would begin to learn the secrets that Scardia's rulers had kept for centuries.

My thoughts were brought back to the present by a harsh slap assaulting my cheek.

'Worthless girl!' My landlady snarled, her red-rimmed eyes blazing with fury. 'Why can't you stop daydreaming and start doing your job?'

The abruptness of the slap had shaken the shawl around my hair and, as I hit the bar, a wisp of hair fell out of my bun. The red fell across my face, and I could taste the faint trace of cranberries on my lips. I pushed the hair back behind my ear, and turned away from the curious gaze of the group of men. The leader was staring at me, eyes blazing with an uncomfortable intensity. It made me feel awkward, and paranoid that he might have seen the hint of white in my hair. Did he realise that the princess he had been talking about was right before his eyes, in a bedraggled and stained gown? I prayed to the Gods of the Sky and Sea that he hadn't.

'This has been happening too frequently of late,' Mrs Jenkins was saying, unaware that I was barely listening, 'I won't stand for it any longer. All winter you've been here, and half of the spring too and there has been no improvement whatsoever. You have the rest of the night to get packed but at first light tomorrow, you are leaving here.'

I had been here all winter and half of the spring? Why hadn't I realised before? Normally I would be already gone by this time, I had broken my second rule. How could I have done that? I couldn't be this slack again, especially now the Tracking parties had increased. If I wasn't careful he'd find me, and who knew what terrible punishments the Usurper would bestow on Scardia's last remaining member of the royal family.

'Karliah, girl, are you listening to me?' Her face was an inch from mine, red and sweaty, crooked teeth bared in a grimace.

I ducked my head, 'Yes, Ma'am.' The horrifying visage withdrew slightly and I felt a couple of coppers being put in my hand.

'Here's your wages for the last month,' Mrs Jenkins snapped, 'now go.'

I fled from behind the bar, the gazes of the customers, and, in particular the beady stares of Lisette and Keely following me. The coppers were clasped tightly in my fist, and I peeked at them, realising that they barely covered half of my monthly wage. This was so unfair.

I took the stairs two at a time and shut my door behind me as quietly as possible. Now that I was alone I felt the tears start to well behind my closed eyes. I took a few deep, steadying breaths, got myself back under control and began packing my bag with the few possessions I had. I preferred to travel light, which was helpful if I had to make a hasty escape, though luckily that had not had to happen frequently. The few coppers in my hand were placed amongst my other ragged dress and holey stockings. The stained scarf came off my head and was placed on top, wrapping everything into a bundle.

The only garment that I had bothered to take care of was my cloak, which now just lightly skimmed the ground. I had grown into it, as I'm sure Lyn had foreseen when she chose it, so now it fit perfectly. As I picked it up the comforting aroma of pine needles and freshly turned earth filled the air, and I held the fabric close, relishing the moment of peace. I barely noticed my hair come out of the bun and fall down to the nape of my back. All that mattered was the second of comfort and tranquillity that only my cloak could provide.

The cloak had originally been my father's. As a young girl I remember him wearing it whenever he went out riding: a billowing cloud of black that followed him like a shadow as he rode into the forest to hunt. And when he returned he would reach down and place me before him in the saddle, laughing as I squealed in delight. I could no longer remember the sound of his voice or the comforting touch of his hand on my shoulder, and that knowledge cut deeper than any knife. The tears that I had been holding back broke forth and ran down my cheeks. I clutched the cloak tighter, desperate for the security it reminded me of.

There was a light cough from the doorway and I jumped, spinning to notice Keely shifting uncomfortably from foot to foot. Lisette was perched on his shoulder and regarded me with glinting eyes.

'Are you alright?' Keely asked, edging forward.

'How long have you been standing there?' I demanded, furious with myself for a momentary lapse of weakness. I was sure that I'd closed the door, but how could I have forgotten to lock it? 'You had no right to come in. Get out.'

Keely was taken aback at my ferocity, and I heard Lisette click her beak. They hadn't ever seen me lose my temper, I realised, for I preferred to act timidly and meekly around other people. But his being in my room was dangerous – what if he noticed my hair?

My hair. Oh by the Gods, it was undone. I knew it would look too suspicious to cover it now, so hoped and prayed that he would leave before noticing the obvious cranberry streak.

'I heard you crying,' he said, 'and I thought it was because of you being thrown out so sudden.'

Suddenly, I corrected silently, as I wiped my cheeks dry with the back of my hand. There was no chance that he would catch me crying again.

'I wanted to see how you were after she hit you,' he continued, and I felt a stab of shame for being so rude. 'And to make sure that you have somewhere to go tomorrow. It's not right for a woman to travel alone, at least, not with the Trackers and bandits on the roads these days.'

I was touched. But not enough to stay in Little Fleming. I had been here for nearly five months, which was far too long.

'I've been fine before, Keely,' I said firmly, as I walked over to the door, preparing to close it in his face. 'I'm touched that you care enough to check how I am, but I'm fine. I've been taking care of myself for long enough to know how to deal with these things.' I indicated the red mark that had bloomed on my cheek. 'Thank you for your concern, but I will be alright tomorrow. I have a place to go.' This was a lie, but Keely didn't need to know that. This false security would calm his mind, and let him say goodbye with a clear conscience, under the impression that I would be safe.

'Where?'

Damn, why was he so inquisitive? And, more importantly, why did he *care?*

'Um,' I searched my mind for a moment, trying to locate the name of a town, any town, 'Turfsdon.'

'Turfsdon?' He asked sceptically, raising an eyebrow. 'Really?'

'Yes,' I replied quickly, 'Turfsdon.' My hand was on the door, ready to push it closed. Lisette squawked as Keely reached forwards and touched my hair. I recoiled, stepping back, terrified. No one had touched my hair since the Dark Time.

'Your hair is real pretty,' he said, but I could tell that he was confused by my reaction. In an instant I was back by the door, and closing it.

'Thank you,' my voice was tight, restrained.

Lisette landed on my head and I felt a tug. A low cry escaped me and I saw Keely's eyes widen as Lisette dropped a hair into his hand. A hair whose light covering of juice had now faded, revealing the pure white beneath.

Chapter Two

There was no time to waste. I slammed the door shut, locked it and turned to grab my bundle. In an instant I had crossed the room and opened my window. The night air was cool as I placed my pack on the roof tiles and prepared to follow it myself. I turned around, checking quickly that I hadn't forgotten anything.

Outside the door Keely was silent, until there was a light knock. When I didn't reply, he knocked harder, turned the handle and realised that I had locked the door.

'Karliah?' He said, 'please open up.'

I let out a quiet breath and vaulted out of the window, landing silently on the tiles. With shaking fingers, I picked up my bag and slung it across my shoulder, whilst tying the cloak under my chin. The hood fell over my head, masking my hair and face, as I crept across the roof as stealthily as possible.

I was sure that he would try to break the door down and discover that I had escaped. Would he follow me or go straight to the nearest Tracker Tower and let them know that the missing princess was fleeing Little Fleming?

I didn't want to know: all that mattered was that I get away as soon as possible. My foot slipped on a tile and I began falling, plummeting towards the ground. If the group of men leaving the inn had not exited at that exact moment, then my story would have ended then and there. Instead I shrieked, and hit the tallest one, knocking him to the ground.

'What on earth…?' The others began, as I lay in the mud, gasping for breath. The man I had knocked over looked at me, and I thanked the gods that he had not been too badly hurt. Shocked, maybe, but not hurt.

'Wait a moment,' one of the men was saying, 'isn't she the girl from the inn?'

'I am so sorry,' I whispered to the man I had hit, 'so very sorry.' There was a commotion from above and Keely poked his head out of my bedroom window. He had knocked down the door, then. Adrenaline gave me strength and I leapt to my feet, backing away from the group of men who were all leaning down to help their friend up. Keely saw me and called out something, but the sound of my pounding heart filled my ears as I sprinted away, so I never heard what he said.

The steady thump of my feet hitting the cobbles helped me to concentrate on what had happened. My chest hurt as I tried to breathe, but I ran on, determined to put as much distance as possible between myself and the inn. The sooner I got to the stables, the better. Once there, I could mount Dolce and go.

My silent curses filled my mind, how could I have been so stupid? In one night all of my three rules had been broken. Who knew what would happen now, now that someone else knew my secret? There would be no point in denying anything, because my flight only highlighted the truth of my identity.

Had the group of men noticed anything suspicious apart from my toppling from the roof of the inn? It had been too dark for them to notice the colour of my hair, although they would have been confused by my sudden departure. I had to admit, I couldn't have chosen a more inconspicuous method of leaving.

So much for remaining discreet.

I paused for a moment, wheezing painfully on the bridge in the centre of Little Fleming. The small river flowed beneath me, lapping softly against the banks. The clouds had parted and the stars twinkled, winking to me in the night sky. Apart from the harsh sound of my breathing, everything around me was tranquil. But in the distance I could hear someone calling out my name, not my pseudonym, but my real name.

'Milady Nina! Wait!'

In that instant the tranquillity was broken and a cold sweat broke out over my body. I forced my feet to move, stumbling towards the dark stables at the end of the street. I cursed Keely as I entered to the musty smell of horse and hay. Of all things, he had to use my real name. If he had wanted there to be even a slim chance that I would stop and listen to him, he had lost it now. There was no way that I would stay now.

Dolce was in the stall furthest from the door and I walked towards her, trying to calm myself so that I didn't wake the other horses or scare her. It took a lot longer than I would have liked to prepare her for our departure, since time was of the essence and I couldn't bear to waste a moment. My hands shook slightly as I tightened the straps on the saddle and led her out of the stall. With the help of a mounting block, I sat astride her and began leaving the stable.

I couldn't trust Keely. Who knew how large a reward he would receive from the Usurper if he handed me in. Of this much I was certain: if he caught me and turned me over to the Usurper then he would be given enough gold to see him live in luxury for several lifetimes. Even an honest man would hesitate at this ostentatious reward, and there was no way that I wanted to put Keely to that test.

Dolce began to trot and I wound my hands in her mane, muttering silent but necessary prayers under my breath. Lyn had always told me that one must ask the Gods' favour before setting out on a journey. Their blessing would guarantee safe travel and, with the current situation, there was no way that I wanted to risk avoiding that. If I had had more time before departing, I would have made a small offering to the Gods of the wind and fortune. A small sprinkling of crushed foxglove petals or mint leaves would ensure that all went well. But alas that offering would have to be overlooked. Hopefully the Gods would understand, and be content with my prayers.

It wasn't fair, I thought to myself. I had finally found a town where I could become invisible, a place where I could disappear entirely from human existence. Why did my cover have to be blown, just when I had started to believe that I was disappearing from memory? If only the Usurper hadn't sent out more Trackers, thus highlighting the fact that I was still alive. It made me more vulnerable than ever before.

I should be glad that I hadn't been caught. True, there had been quite a few close shaves in the past, where Trackers had been hot on my trail and I had eluded them. But this was different. Now that I was older, I could stand up against the Usurper and try to reclaim the kingdom but after all the years of hiding and running, the idea of taking that responsibility was too heavy a burden to contemplate.

Dolce halted, shying away from something ahead, and snorted uncomfortably. Something was fluttering around her head, pecking mercilessly at the wispy mane. I caught a glimpse of green feathers and groaned.

'Lisette, go away.' I swatted at the budgie, who darted just out of reach and continued to torment my horse. In vain, I tried to urge Dolce forward but she stood firm, terrified of the vicious presence flitting around her head.

I could hear distant footsteps now, steadily gaining on me. My heart started to pound even louder and the shaking hands that clutched the reins were sweaty. Dolce shied again, faltering before Lisette's onslaught.

Angrily, I dismounted and led Dolce by the reins, swatting away the pestering budgie. With me in front of her, Dolce calmed down enough to walk in a straight line, tail and ears flicking in annoyance at Lisette's pesky chirping. I made soothing noises to ease Dolce even more and fixed my gaze on the horizon. Our progress out of the township was inexorably slow; it would only be a matter of time before Keely caught up with us.

My breaths kept coming short and fast, so it was hard to think properly as my head started to spin. Dolce's head butted me gently and I realised that I'd stopped walking, and that my clenched hands were white, the knuckles garishly outlined in the moonlight. A loud chirp made my eyes glance up from Dolce's neck, and see Lisette perching on the saddle, watching me beadily. She chirped again and ruffled her feathers in the chilly air, before falling into expectant silence.

Silence.

I stood frozen, holding my breath, trying and failing to hear the footsteps that dogged my own. There was nothing remotely humanoid that I could distinguish behind Dolce in the darkness. That could only mean one thing.

Dolce butted me again, urging me to turn around to face the road ahead of us, to face the man I could sense kneeling behind me. With a deep, steadying breath, I turned and regarded Keely's bowed head.

'Forgive me for scaring you, Milady,' he began, and I was surprised to hear the sincerity in his voice. Could it really be possible that he wouldn't do what so many others had done, and haul me off to the nearest guardhouse to claim the bounty? My heart now was pounding not with fear, but hope.

'I just couldn't believe it was really you, Milady,' he continued, 'we all thought you was dead.'

Were, I corrected silently before touching his shoulder gently, helping him to his feet. Keely's eyes were still downcast, and I finally found my tongue.

'Keely,' my voice was slightly raspy from the events of the night, and I swallowed, 'look at me, please.' He acquiesced, raising his eyes to meet my gaze steadily. I was still shaking and held onto Dolce's saddle to steady myself. 'Why did you follow me, Keely?' A note of steel entered my voice, but he didn't flinch.

'You was alone,' he said and I had to grit my teeth to stop correcting him, 'and you didn't know where to go, it was obvious from when I asked you. Plus, you're the princess, so you need to be protected. Trackers are everywhere, not to mention what you could stumble across in the wilderness.'

'I've taken care of myself since the Dark Time, Keely,' I replied, slowly, patiently, hoping that he would understand that I would rather travel alone. If on the odd chance I got caught, I didn't want Keely to get taken away with me. The punishment for a Scardian royal was bad enough, but what would they do to people who helped a fugitive? A part of me cringed, remembering witnessing what had happened to people who had tried to shelter me before. By my ninth summer I realised that it was better to travel alone, I couldn't bear the thought of ruining people's lives, especially well-meaning, kind people. Like Keely.

Keely hadn't moved, he stood, resolute, watching me intently. Something in his expression scared me, an intensity which I hadn't glimpsed there before.

'Begging your pardon, milady,' he said, ducking his head, 'but I *am* going with you. I saw you when you arrived in this town, and I saw your expression tonight when you was about to leave it. Perhaps you think that you can continue like you have these past years. But you're nearly eighteen: the Usurper is looking for you, and you need to get away until he grows lax and forgetful.'

I didn't know which surprised me more, that Keely was able to read my mind or that he had used 'lax' in a sentence. He was smarter than I had given him credit for.

Shocked, I just stood there, nodding slowly. Perhaps it wouldn't be *that* bad having someone else with me. Two pairs of eyes were better than one, the saying went. After all, Keely would make a good bodyguard, of that I was certain, after watching him for the past few months keeping the peace at the inn.

'Alright,' I said, and a cold hand clutched at my heart: was I making the right decision?

Keely grinned and clicked his tongue. From the closely-knit trees on the side of the road, a shaggy horse stepped forward, a roughly tied pack on its saddle, dark eyes glistening in the moonlight. With agility I never would have expected him to possess, Keely leapt into the saddle and wound his hands around the reins before looking at me expectantly.

'Where to?' He asked at the same moment I said,

'You planned this.'

We looked at each other for a moment in silence before he smiled and I bit my cheek to prevent myself following suit.

Instead I remounted Dolce and nudged her forward, till we were riding side by side. Then I repeated myself.

'You planned this, Keely. Your following me wasn't a moment of thoughtlessness. You *knew* I'd run here. You *prepared* to stop me here. And,' I indicated to his pack, 'you *knew* I'd relent and let you come with me.'

'*Protect* you,' Keely corrected, still smiling, 'and yes, I did plan it. I've been planning it awhile. I had my suspicions you see,' he tapped his temple, a knowing glint in his eye, 'I had them from the moment you walked through that inn door, and after that I only became more and more certain.I knew it would only be a matter of time before you ran for it, so I kept Nancy stabled behind the inn and followed you. I packed last night, and when tonight came I was prepared. We cut through the forest to reach you, we did.' He patted Nancy's neck affectionately, 'in fact we—'

'Hang on a moment,' I held up a hand, not caring about how rude I was, 'you didn't go through the forest on the side of town. You ran after me.'

Keely's eyes clouded over with confusion and he shook his head slowly. The cold that had clamped itself around my heart pierced my veins, reaching with icy tendrils through my body from the roots of my hair to the tips of my toes.With a harsh tug on Dolce's mane I turned, zigzagging along the path, just in time to avoid the crossbow bolt that shot through the space where I had just been.

'The forest!' I cried, lying low on Dolce's back, clinging onto her for dear life, hair flicking painfully across my face. Keely got the hint and disappeared within moments into the trees, and I quickly followed.

Branches tugged at me, pulling and catching on every article of clothing, every hair that was exposed. Ahead of me

I heard Keely charging onwards, forging our path, not caring about anything save one: flight.

Another bolt hit a tree trunk to my right, as another whistled past my ear, grazing it before plummeting to the ground. I glanced around wildly, how many Trackers *were* there? A shadowy figure moved behind a tree, bending down, fumbling with something. A movement to my left, another dark silhouette, this one raising a crossbow, and watching me down its sight. The bolt shot forward and in that split second I pulled the knife from where it was hidden in my boot and slashed the air, slicing the quivering bolt in two. The two fragments fell into the remnants of the forest floor that Dolce was kicking behind us. When the next bolt flew towards us I was more prepared, and deflected it with a thrust of the knife, looking around, ready for yet more arrows. Nothing more came, and I sighed with relief.

Heart pounding, I moved ahead, the knife gripped tightly in one hand, the other one caught up in Dolce's mane, directing her back and forth between the trees. In front of us the trees were thinning, the moonlight brightening, Keely and Nancy burst out of the wood with Dolce and I in hot pursuit. The two horses churned up the ground beneath us as we raced through the field of knee-high grass, leaving the forest behind.

'You don't think they had horses, do you, Milady Nina?' Keely gasped, and I had to strain to catch the words before they were carried away by the wind. I saw his gaze lower and widen on seeing the knife in my hand. Self-consciously, I pushed it back into the leather sheath on the inside of my boot. My mind was spinning, tossing up different possibilities as to how they'd found me.

'I don't think so,' I replied, surprisingly my voice was somewhat calmer than what I felt inside: a trembling, wobbly mess. 'We would have heard something by now if they had been prepared to follow us.' As I spoke, I glanced behind at the forest, which blocked the last view of Little Fleming. There was no sign of any disturbance among the trees, no sign of any crossbowmen under their boughs, watching our escape. A shiver went down my spine, and I urged Dolce to go faster, wanting to put as much distance as possible between us and our attackers.

In that moment I didn't care about Keely keeping pace with us, only about flight. Who knew how long it would be before more Trackers were on our trail? Would they bring dogs to hunt us down? It was only a matter of time before they would be pouring into the inn and interrogating Mrs Jenkins about me. Who knew what she would say when confronted with the truth, that I had been lying for the past few months, pretending to be someone who was the epitome of normal. No doubt she would waste no time in telling the Trackers how useless I had been as a barmaid, how I was an unreliable girl, who had not enough money to see me through the spring rains. That knowledge would ease their minds, the belief that I would not be able to support myself and that it would not take long for me to return to one of the nearby villages. I was certain that by this time tomorrow, this whole area would be swarming with Trackers, all hoping to catch my scent.

'We need to get as far away as possible,' I told Keely, 'do you know this area well?'

'I only came here a few years back,' Keely grunted as he tugged Nancy's head away from a branch of fresh green leaves. 'The nearest town is two miles east if we follow the

Tribor Road. We can cut back towards it over the Old Bridge at Fieldhaven.'

'I don't think it's wise to travel by road, Keely,' I replied, 'by tomorrow Trackers will have overrun everywhere within a ten-mile radius of Little Fleming. It'll be too dangerous to travel by the Tribor Road.'

'Then what do you suggest?' Keely's voice was tight, almost as though he anticipated my response before I spoke.

'We go cross-country.' As I spoke, I pictured a map of north western Scardia, contemplating whether we would be able to reach the Lightbringer Mountains by dawn. 'We head for the Lightbringer Mountains, Keely, with all due haste.'

He didn't say anything, just nodded and we urged our steeds onward into the deepening night.

Chapter Three

The Lightbringer Mountains had been discovered and named by Edward Lightbringer, the third leader of Scardia. He, along with a contingent of warriors, had- according to legend- scaled each mountain and slaughtered the fabled Drach-Mah, a deadly creature with three heads and a shaggy hide. Some believed it to resemble a bear, others claimed that it walked on its hind legs like a man. As far as I knew, there had been no sightings of the strange creature in these mountains ever since Edward emerged victorious, holding one of its heads in a gauntlet-clad fist. A statue of this moment had been raised in the Hall of Memories, joining the ranks of other portrayals of Scardia's heroes captured forever in the cold embrace of stone.

Now, almost a millennium later, I stood in awe of the Lightbringer Mountains, frozen for a moment, not due to the biting late winter wind, but at the sheer beauty of the sight. Keely stood next to me, holding onto the horses' reins, while Lisette ruffled her feathers at the cold. We had crossed multiple paddocks and fields, traversed fast flowing streams and always kept out of sight of the roads. The mountains ahead of us rose high towards the heavens, the sky glowing pink in the dawn light.

It was amazing that even though the harsh frosts of winter had dissipated in Little Fleming, which was only several miles away, in these mountains there was still the soft crunch of snow underfoot. In a few weeks, the peaks would begin to thaw and the hand of winter would recede again. Ahead of us the snow stretched far and wide, interrupted occasionally with clusters of boulders or the stiff trunks of silvery trees. I stepped over to one and withdrew my knife, cutting into the bark of a branch. Instead of having sap on the inside, the wood was dry and flaky, breaking easily away from the trunk when I kicked it. I stepped back in dismay, an uncanny sense telling me that all the trees within the mountains would be just like this one: dead.

'Milady Nina,' Keely said, 'where are we heading after this? Do you have a plan at all?'

I shook my head for a moment, before remembering the men in the inn. They'd talked about the Resistance. I should seek them out and find them, maybe even take the first steps towards reclaiming the throne. Surely that would be what my parents would have wanted, it's what the people of Scardia would want, for no one had ever claimed to be completely happy under the Usurper's rule.

'A kingdom won through bloodshed is no victory, but a curse,' my mother had once told me, and now the words rang true in my ears, almost as if she herself stood beside me, whispering them into the wind.

'Milady?' Keely's voice interrupted the brief memory, and I turned in his direction, disorientated for a moment. A strong hand gripped my elbow to steady me, and I realised just how tired I was.

'We should pitch camp soon, Keely,' I said, gently removing his hand from my arm and leaning instead against Dolce for support. 'And please call me Karliah, it's unwise to use anything else.' He nodded briskly and soon had found a small shelter from the wind in a cluster of large rocks. We tied the horses to a dead tree nearby, which was hidden from view of the distant fields. I hoped that the Trackers wouldn't venture this far east today and discover us at the base of the mountains.

Keely cleared our makeshift campsite of any snow, and pulled some dry kindling and flint out of his saddlebag. Within moments he had caused a wisp of smoke to burst into a small flame, which slowly grew stronger with the aid of remnants of branches which we roughly broke off the nearby trees. As there was nothing within the vicinity of our camp that could serve as any sort of food, I scooped up some nearby clean snow and put it into my mouth. It took a few moments for the icy pain to subside, but even longer for the ache behind my eyes to fade.

Keely glanced up at me over the campfire, gazing intently through the sparks that flew as I poked roughly at the flames.

'How did you learn to use a knife?' He asked, 'how long ago was it?'

I pulled the said knife out of its sheath and stroked the flat of the blade, as memories of the past began to unfurl in my mind. Engraved into the metal were two leaves of ivy, twisting and merging together.

'It's a long story, Keely,' I replied, 'one that might be too long to tell over a campfire.'

'Then begin it,' he urged, and I could hear the impatient underlying curiosity in his tone.

I sighed, unsure of how to begin. 'I learnt some basic knife fighting techniques before the Dark Time. The Master of Arms taught me, he was called Jekyll.' A smile tweaked the edges of my lips upward as I remembered the tall unshaven man who had both terrified and intrigued me. His voice had been like a crack of thunder, scaring many of the palace guards into submission. My father never told me where Jekyll came from or how he happened to become the Master of Arms, but he was starkly different to any of the other guards in the palace. Often, he had been uncouth and harsh, yet at other times he had surprising amounts of patience which softened his tough exterior, like when he taught me how to wield a dagger with what I could've sworn had been a smile.

Keely didn't say anything to interrupt my abrupt silence, his chin rested in his hand, and his gaze never wavered from my face. On his shoulder Lisette squawked and ruffled her feathers, and he absentmindedly reached into a pouch at his belt and withdrew a small handful of seeds. In an instant Lisette was perched on his hand, digging into her own repast, which looked more appetising than fresh snow.

'But, Karliah,' Keely said, 'that knife there is no blade that was forged in Scardia. No blacksmith here has the skill to achieve those engravings.'

'It wasn't forged in Scardia, that's true,' I replied, as a more painful memory was brought to mind which I instantly tried to forget, 'it was a gift from the family on my mother's side.'

A strange tightness gripped my throat, cutting me off, for even after all these years it was still hard to talk about my family.

'She came from over the Eastern Sea,' I said, my voice barely audible over the crackle of the fire and the sounds of Lisette eating.

'The Meridian?' Keely was shocked, apparently he had never heard the tale of my parent's union. I nodded.

'Originally, this blade was hers.'

For a moment we were both frozen, staring at the dagger in my hands, each caught up in our own thoughts. The memory I had tried to suppress was threatening to envelop me and, in a hasty attempt to thwart the past, I thrust the knife back into the sheath.

'I think that's enough talk over the campfire for one night,' I murmured, 'we should rest.'

'I'll take the first watch,' Keely said, and I felt a twinge of unease. This could be his chance to alert Trackers to our position and claim the reward. Could I trust him?

But one look at Keely's open face, and Lisette's beady eyes, was enough to ease my worries. He seemed too earnest, too eager to doggedly follow me, to appear hostile. Perhaps I could trust him. Wrapping my cloak tighter around my body, I just nodded my assent and curled into a ball beside the flames, as a wave of fatigue overcame me, casting me almost immediately into the feared realm of dreams, nightmares and memories.

Young hands, my hands, reached up and placed the necklace around my neck. It was heavy, studded with diamonds and rubies, as was the silver circlet that my mother had placed on my head mere hours before. The strings of diamonds fell down and suspended just above my navel, and I admired myself in the polished mirror. But something was missing, and I reached up to slip the matching earrings off the dressing table. My small, eager fingers struggled to put them on. There was a chance yet that I could try to be as beautiful as my mother.

'Nina, what are you doing?'

The voice was light and musical, soft and low, which almost made tears come to my eyes. In the memory I turned, petrified at being caught amongst my mother's jewels. Instead of looking serious or angry, she was biting back a laugh. In two strides, she was standing before me, a tall willowy woman with pale blue eyes and waist length strawberry blonde hair. In my eyes, she was a vision of perfection.

'Mama,' I began, 'I was—'

'Playing dress up?' She asked.

I nodded, lowering my head, and began to finger the strings of diamonds, waiting for my punishment.

'I think that you can wear these when you're older,' my mother smiled, prying the earrings off my ears and lifting the circlet off my brow. It took a bit more effort to remove the necklace, as my fingers clutched tight, unwilling to let go.

'When you have your first ball or when you get married, you can wear these,' my mother said, clearly hoping that this would prove to be incentive enough for me to let go. However, at the age of five, my first ball would be many years away, and so I just clung tighter.

It had often shocked me how my mother could be so unceasingly patient. She surprised me now, and gradually eased the necklace out of my fingers, whispering comforting words which I could barely hear. Within moments I had my arms wrapped around her neck, clinging there instead, and she lifted me up, placing the necklace carefully on her dressing table. Her arms held me there, and I inhaled the musky scent of her perfume. She pressed her lips to my cheek and I shut my eyes, already feeling myself drift away from the moment, moving instead towards the inevitable future.

Now I was seven, and my mother entered my room, her hair a wild mess around her shoulders. Little had changed in two years, save for several worry lines which had appeared on her face, yet now there was a terrified glint in her eyes which was enough to get me out of bed. My mother was never scared.

'Nina, my darling, you must get changed, *immediately.*' No one disobeyed my mother when she spoke in that tone, not even my father. She helped me into some dark clothes before pausing by the door and listening for a moment. It was only then that I realised that the corridors and the courtyard were filled with the sounds of people running, crying out and the clash of swords meeting. Instantly, fear entered my soul and lodged itself in my blood, a place where it would remain for many long years to come.

For a moment my mother hesitated, and then she turned, withdrawing a sheathed dagger from the folds of her gown.

'My father gave this to me before I married your father, Wilhelmina,' she said quickly, and I shuddered at the use of my full name. 'Ever since it has served me well, and now I want you to have it. There is danger here, my darling, and we must escape it, you and I. Come, I told Lyn to meet us near the stables at the foot of the servant's staircase.'

'What about Papa?' I asked, as she led me out into the corridor and looked left and right to perceive any danger.

'He isn't coming, Nina.' Her expression was blank, hiding perhaps the pain which I now knew must've lain in her heart.

'Why not?' I asked.

She swallowed, and pulled my arm tighter, dragging me through the corridors and downstairs. Servants and guards were all around us, moving in every direction, swarming together in a shrieking cacophony. My mother's grip was my only tether to reality as we ran onwards, pushing through the fearful crowd.

'Mama?' My voice was lost in the noise around us, and she made no acknowledgement to show that she had heard me.

'Nina,' she said suddenly, 'if we get separated then you must promise to keep going and meet Lyn. Promise me.'

'Yes, Mama,' I replied, subdued. We raced past a window, and I saw fires lighting up the sky, and silhouettes of men fighting on the battlements of the walls, and falling into the dark abyss below. I bit back a whimper and ran onwards behind my mother, turning corner after corner, dodging between people caught in the frenzy. Ahead of us I saw the entrance to the servants' staircase, through a narrow door at the end of the passageway. From one of the nearby corridors there came the sound of marching feet and the metallic clash of armour and swords. Cries of pain reached my ears, and I shivered, pulling closer to my mother's side.

We reached the door with barely a second to spare before the marching feet rounded the corner and saw us. In that instant my mother pushed me through the door and shut it behind me, leaving me alone beside the servants' staircase.

'Go,' she hissed through the wood. 'Go now!'

Instead of obeying, I pressed myself against the keyhole and watched, terrified as my mother waited for the men to approach.

'So, Queen Lydia, we meet again.' The voice was rough and made me bite my lip in fear.

'Indeed we do, Lord Niall.' My mother's voice was cold, and I could imagine her steely gaze. 'Yet again it seems you have shown not only a lack of decorum but also how low your character has sunk. By what right do you cross our threshold? I believe that we were very clear with you the last time we spoke.'

'And you were, madam,' the man replied, 'yet it seems you are yet to learn that when I request something, I get it.'

'You dare—' My mother began, but Lord Niall stepped forward too quickly and pulled a blade close to her throat.

'Where is your pretty little daughter this evening, Lydia?'
His voice was low and menacing.

'You beast,' she retorted, 'you'll never find her.'

'You underestimate me and the influence I hold,' he said.
My mother replied by spitting in his face. He roared and drew
the blade across her throat, before kicking her fallen body to
the edge of the corridor.

'Let's find the bitch and put an end to her,' he growled to
his guards, and they strode away.

I pressed my nails into my palms until they hurt, so that
the tears on the edge of my vision wouldn't fall. Through the
keyhole I saw my mother's body quiver and then go limp,
blood pooling around her. I wanted to run to her, to hold her
body and scream and cry.

'Mama,' I whispered brokenly, fighting back tears. 'Mama.'

This hadn't been what I wanted when I made my wish.

Chapter Four

The sharp light of the sun roused me from my slumber. With a muffled groan, I turned over and saw to my horror that Keely was slumped against one of the boulders, lightly snoring. So much for keeping watch!

In a moment I was up and covering the fire with snow, I wondered if the loud hiss from the embers would wake him. He twitched in his sleep and then grunted something under his breath, but it seemed that he had no intention whatsoever of awakening.

I peered over the edges of the boulders that had made up our camp, checking to see if there were any signs of life either within or outside of the mountains. Nothing moved in my field of vision, save Lisette, who had fluttered onto a dead tree, watching me keenly.

It was time to go. There might not be any Trackers now, but I knew they would come.

'Keely,' I said, walking over to Dolce's side and stroking her neck with the back of my hand. Keely didn't even stir. Sighing impatiently, I strode to his side and shook his arm roughly.

'We need to move out, Keely.'

'Karliah, be a love and put the tea on,' he muttered in his sleep. I shook him again, before kicking his leg into the snow.

On coming into contact with the freezing wet snow, he jumped awake with a jerk and a sharp cry, which I instantly muffled by clasping a hand over his mouth. Lisette squawked and flew at me, blinding me in a wave of green feathers. Keely bit down hard and I stifled a yelp but clung on tighter, until the sleepiness had completely faded from his eyes. When he'd stopped struggling, I pulled away and mounted Dolce.

'We have to go, Keely,' I repeated, 'now.'

'What about breakfast?' He asked, as he mounted Nancy, a grumpy Lisette settling on his shoulder. I almost laughed at the notion.

'We don't have time,' I replied, 'although if you want fresh snow, go ahead and help yourself.'

He scrunched up his face in distaste and dejectedly gathered a handful of snow which soon disappeared into his mouth. I bit back a smile at his expression, and nudged Dolce forwards, not waiting for Keely to follow. Within moments he was alongside me, rubbing a hand over his bleary eyes.

Ahead of us the path was uneven and rocky, with scattered patches of snow and ice. I gritted my teeth, because if we were going to try to hide our tracks by walking around the snowdrifts, then our progress would be painfully slow. Perhaps the Trackers would reach the Lightbringer Mountains before we had even traversed them.

'It's awfully quiet,' Keely commented, as he gazed around at the bleak terrain. 'No birds, no mice: nothing. It's unnatural.'

Lisette gave a small squawk of agreement and ruffled her feathers. In response, Keely placed her on his shoulder where she nestled into his hair. I turned away, baffled. There would be no way that I would ever allow a budgerigar to snuggle into my neck, for fear of being bitten by a sharp beak.

'You're right,' I said, and shivered. The steady sound of hoofbeats and our breath in the frozen air contrasted drastically with the silence, and I almost felt like it was criminal. For a while Keely was silent, and I was able to lose myself in my thoughts. Images from my dreams the previous night threatened to intrude on my mind, and in a desperate attempt to evade them, I began to hum a tune that my mother had sung over my bedside.

That low lilting tune had often subdued my tears and eased me into slumber, and now it enclosed me once again in a sense of blissful serenity. So engrossed in my thoughts was I, that I did not hear the subtle noises that reached Keely's ears.

'Karliah?' I ignored his voice, and looked ahead at the empty road, wondering how long it would be before we reached the end of the pass. Where would we go from there? Would the Trackers be close behind us? Or would they have sent out messenger hawks, to alert the Usurper and their comrades that they had caught my trail?

'Karliah!' Keely hissed, reaching out to grasp my shoulder. My instant reaction was to shake him off and turn to glare at him.

'What?' I snapped waspishly, still having not completely forgiven him for falling asleep during his watch last night. He raised a finger to his lips, and then indicated the snow-covered slopes around us. I followed his gaze, and noticed some patches that were a different shade from the rest. It seemed to be shifting, moving slightly, almost as though the ground were breathing in a long slow rhythm.

'What do you think it is?' I asked, my voice hushed, eager to not disturb the silence any more than we already had. It couldn't be Trackers, for they had never resorted to using camouflage, nor could it be bandits, for surely they would have taken advantage of attacking us while we slept.

Keely shrugged as we began to edge forward, gradually distancing ourselves from the strange disturbance in the snow. As we moved away, it became increasingly clear that whatever was in the snow was alive. Sounds began to break the stillness of the pass, light grunts and snuffles which made me more eager to leave it behind us.

'I think it must be coming out of some kind of hibernation,' Keely murmured, and I looked at him, confused.

'But what kind of animal hibernates in *snow*?' I asked, 'I thought most hibernated in caves or whatnot, so as to avoid the cold.'

Keely paused for a moment, and we both froze as the creature behind us seemed to shift, sending the snow down onto the track in a thick trail of sludge. We turned, and I covered my mouth to stop myself crying out.

Where there had been an oddly patched mountainside of snow, there now was a bizarrely shaped creature that was shaking the snow off its furry coat. It almost looked like a cross between a bear and a bull, with thick paws which were almost swallowed up in the snow.

'It couldn't be,' Keely muttered, 'it's impossible.'

'What's impossible?' I didn't like having to constantly ask questions like this, it made me feel like my grip on control was slipping away and I wouldn't be able to regain it. I liked knowing things first, telling others about them, not being constantly required to ask questions like a child.

'The Drach-Mah.' Keely's voice was awed, almost reverent.

I looked at the creature that was now stamping its clawed feet into the ground, grunting as it did a final shake of its hide. Certainly, it had the thick coat that the legends spoke of, and the terrifying size. But there was one problem, which did not concur with the story I had been raised on.

'It only has one head.' I commented, feeling increasingly stupid as the words left my mouth, and even more so when Keely turned to look at me, eyebrows raised. 'The story of Edward Lightbringer and the Drach-Mah clearly states that the Drach-Mah was terrorising the neighbouring provinces and was a fearsome three-headed beast that walked on four and two legs. That creature there,' I pointed towards it, 'doesn't appear to be violent or terrifying, save to the salmon in the nearest river.'

Keely smiled at my fumbled explanation and I scowled. It wasn't my fault that I had never learnt how to adequately express myself clearly. Beneath me, Dolce came to an abrupt halt and I turned to face the rocky path before us, my hands were gripping the reins and my heart gave a sudden thud of shock. Keely, following my gaze, let out a hiss of surprise, the air forming a mist around his face before fading into nothingness.

'Who is she?' He whispered.

I only shook my head in reply. My gaze couldn't leave the woman who stood only twenty paces away. She looked almost familiar, and yet uncannily fey, but I felt that I should recognise her.

'Isn't she cold?' Keely muttered, for she was wearing neither fur nor cloak, only a simple robe, which almost made her blend into the snow, like the Drach-Mah had. Her hair was white blond and fluttering in wisps around her face, but her unblinking eyes didn't seem to be bothered by it.

She stood there, a figure blocking our path, yet making no attempt to hold us back or speak to us. What bothered me was how she had gotten there so quickly. If she had been travelling from the opposite end of the pass, we might have seen her. Instead, she had just appeared, as if from thin air.

There was no point in standing around and letting the cold sap our strength away. If she had something to say to us, no doubt she would say it. With a gentle nudge, Dolce stepped forward. Nancy, as if taking courage from her, followed suit, although staying a few paces behind in case some catastrophe occurred.

The woman's eyes were riveted on me and followed our slow progress from twenty paces to ten, and then to five. When we were within speaking distance, she held up a hand and the two horses stopped. In close quarters I could see that her skin was nearly translucent, the veins were pronounced and it seemed that with one gust of wind she would topple and be blown away. Her sharply angular face looked up at us, and I realised what she was waiting for.

My hands shook slightly as I dismounted and turned to face her. On the ground I realised how tall she was and wished that I had stayed in Dolce's saddle. At least up there I had felt safe. Now I was all too aware of the snuffles and grunts from the Drach-Mah behind us, and the cold, calm gaze of woman before us. Keely's reassuring grip held my elbow, and I felt a small wave of gratitude. I had forgotten what it felt like to have someone support me when I was travelling.

'Who are you?' I asked, thankful that my voice didn't waver as I strove to meet her gaze.

She didn't reply for several moments, but held her hand out, palm up, and captured a snowflake. Keely and I glanced upward, surprised: it hadn't been snowing when we set off, and there hadn't been any clouds that would forewarn snow.

The woman seemed to be amused at our confusion, the corners of her thin mouth crinkled upwards for half a second.

'It is unwise to be travelling at this time of year, Wilhelmina.' Her voice was light and airy, almost like the snowflakes that were now floating around us.

'How do you know my name?' I asked. 'Who are you?'

'I know all,' she replied, 'the Winter Spirit knows everything. From the whispered confidences over a campfire to the cooks preparing a sumptuous feast for Scardia's nobles, nothing escapes my notice.'

For a moment I was speechless, unsure of how to continue.

'You're one of the seasonal spirits,' Keely said, 'a God.'

The Winter Spirit held up a slender hand, 'not quite a God. My siblings and I do not hold that honour. We merely herald the seasons and stay until they reach their end.'

'You were known by another name once though,' I murmured, as the old story formed once again in my mind.

'Indeed I was,' she replied. 'But I'm afraid I cannot go into details about that with you mortals now. Time is running short. There are only seven months until you turn eighteen, Wilhelmina. Lord Niall will be following up on any rumour of you during this time, and so you must go somewhere safe. You must leave Scardia and return to the land of your mother's people. They can protect you and teach you what you must know before your eighteenth birthday. There is a resistance building there. That is where you must go; it is too dangerous for you to stay in Scardia.'

'Why do you care so much?' I asked, despite Keely's nervous glance. 'If you cared about me being safe for so long, why didn't some Season Spirit come to tell me years ago?'

'You might have died.' Her tone was flat and cold, making me shiver. 'You weren't ready nor worthy. You had to learn how to live without the aid of friends or family. A future queen of Scardia must know her subjects and must have known hunger, cold and sleeping under the stars. She must be able to empathise and trust her own judgement in the face of fire.'

Her words were making me nervous, reminding me of who I really was and what had always been expected of me. No amount of wishing could make that go away.

The icy touch of her fingers against my cheek, forcing me to look at her, made me jump.

'I know what you fear and what haunts you.' I knew almost instantly that these words were for me and me alone, Keely would not be able to hear them. 'The pain will fade as will the fear. In time you will heal, but only after you have fulfilled your destiny and faced the demons that haunt your past.'

'I'm afraid,' I whispered, 'I do not think I should rule. I'm not like my parents were; I don't think I can do it.'

The Winter Spirit smiled and stepped away.

'The hard frost must melt and change to allow the grass to grow,' she said, 'the snow must go to allow the spring to come. And so must you, my dear.'

Keely glanced between us, confused, and I shook my head. He shrugged and mounted Nancy, and I followed suit. The Winter Spirit was now no longer blocking our path, preferring to stand next to me.

'Those who follow you are not far behind,' she warned, 'I can keep them at bay for as long as my brother allows.' She indicated to the creature who was snuffling behind us, nosing its way up a snowy slope.

'The Drach-Mah?' Keely asked.

'The Drach-Mah died at the hands of your ancestor,' the Winter Spirit said to me, 'that's my brother, the Lord of

Springtime. He will only allow you a day before he dismantles my roadblock. Go now.'

Without another word she walked away, and I urged Dolce onwards, but turned to peer behind us at the spirit's retreating back. The sky darkened and a static energy began to fill the air, as elemental power was unleashed on the path behind us. Our horses, scared of the sudden noise, needed no urging to go faster and soon we were putting the landslide of ice and snow behind us.

'Did I hear her right,' Keely said, 'that the Trackers are close behind us *and* we only have one day to broaden that distance?'

'Too true,' I replied, still quite flustered after the strange meeting. It had reinforced the things I ran from, and the fears I had of going back. It was strange to realise that the spirits had been watching me all my life and knew my every move. They were worse than the Usurper's Trackers, who were at least paid for it. The spirits did it for enjoyment, waiting until the proper time to intervene and announce their presence.

'How long should it take for us to get out of here?' Keely asked, and I shrugged. Who knew. Maybe the Winter Spirit would guide our path and make us reach the end of the pass more quickly.

'What was she once called?' He said, 'you said that she was known as somethin' other than the Winter Spirit in a time long passed.'

'Didn't you ever hear the ancient lore of Scardia?' I asked, 'maybe when you sat on your grandmother's knee?' As I said it, I could picture it. An old woman and a young boy, who was followed by a faithful menagerie of cats, dogs or birds, sitting next to a warm hearth on a winter's night. To my chagrin, Keely shook his head.

'My grandmother died before I was born,' he said, 'and my parents were not the sort of people who would consider the country's lore of any importance.'

For a moment I was speechless, unable to think of anything to say. How could I have automatically assumed that his upbringing would have been slightly similar to mine?

'She was known as the Ice Queen,' I said. 'But here isn't the place to talk about it.'

Chapter Five

It was not long before we had reached the end of the pass, and I wondered at how quickly we had travelled in such a short time. Maybe the Winter Spirit had indeed lessened the distance that we had needed to cross; although how such a feat would be achieved I had no idea. We paused for a moment to look back at the Lightbringer Mountains and I wondered if I'd ever have a reason to go through the pass again. What would it be like to build a small hut on one of the slopes and, on clear days, have a view of the vast forests and rivers of Scardia?

'Look, Karliah,' Keely said, and pointed at a lumbering animal that was gradually getting closer. As it drew nearer, I realised that it was the Lord of Spring.

I dismounted and took a sip from my water skin, before returning it to my saddlebags. Within moments the spirit was mere inches away from me, and I bowed in acknowledgement.

'Thank you,' I said, and privately sent out another thanks to the Winter Spirit. Without their help we would probably be encircled by Trackers by now.

The Lord of Spring leaned his horned head against my right shoulder and my mind was filled with images. I gasped and the pictures began to solidify: a group of men on horseback all wearing black, the two turnings of the sun across the sky and the mountain pass being clear of any landslide, almost as though the Winter Spirit had never created one.

'You're giving us an extra day?' I asked, awed. The Lord snorted and shook his heavily matted coat, before turning and slowly making his way back towards the mountains.

'Thank you, again,' I murmured to his retreating back.

'How do you suppose a creature like that would get rid of that landslide?' Keely asked as I remounted and we set off again.

'No idea,' I said, 'maybe he'll call on the elements like the Winter Spirit did. I can hardly imagine that he'll bother with moving it physically.'

'I guess not.' He said, 'you said that we was getting two days to get a head start on the Trackers.'

I almost corrected him but bit my tongue to stop myself.

'Yes,' I replied, forcing myself to think about what we had to do now, 'We need to go east.'

'There ought to be a town nearby,' Keely said, 'we can get supplies for the journey, or,' he added on seeing my grimace, 'I can go and get some while you remain hidden.'

Although I was all too keen to remain inconspicuous, I still didn't trust Keely enough to let him leave me behind and vulnerable. I couldn't run the risk of him losing his nerve and alerting the Trackers of my presence. It still concerned me how quickly they had found me in Little Fleming.

'No,' I said quickly, and when I met Keely's eyes I had to look away, it was like he'd been able to read my thoughts. The expression on his face almost filled me with shame.

'Alright then,' Keely said, and for a few moments we were silent as we followed the rough track through the clumps of heather and grass. The silence lengthened awkwardly, and eventually my stomach rumbled loudly, reminding me of the lack of breakfast and lunch.

'Do you *have* any food?' Keely asked, and I shook my head.

'I wasn't exactly prepared to leave Little Fleming last night,' I snapped, 'it was because of *you* that I left in such a hurry. If you hadn't scared me then I could have gotten some food before leaving.'

'But instead you slipped out of your window, jumped off the roof and nearly killed a man, before running to the stables.' Keely's voice was expressionless.

What could I say to that?

'You scared me,' I said, 'and I panicked.' Keely didn't say anything, but I felt the need to explain. 'It wasn't the first time someone has recognised me and I had to run without warning.'

'Well you can't keep drawing attention to yourself,' he said, and I blinked at the annoyance in his voice. 'That Spirit was right: you're turning eighteen soon and the Trackers will be hunting for you now more than ever. You can't keep being reckless and drawing attention to yourself like you did at Little Fleming. If you want to survive, you need to find people who can protect you.'

I felt like a child, being chastised for breaking a vase or drawing creatures in charcoal on the wall. Luckily Keely didn't notice my glower cast in his direction, but what right had he to reprimand me for my behaviour? He'd barely known me for a season and already he seemed to think that he knew best how to ensure my safety.

'I'm not a child, Keely,' I snapped, still bristling from his insinuations. 'In the next town we'll stop for supplies and follow the Eastern Way. The further we get from Little Fleming and the Lightbringer Mountains, the better.'

'Very well,' Keely's voice was tight and closed, and I didn't want to talk anymore. I'd rarely seen him lose his temper and I didn't want to push him to that point. However, to my surprise, he drew a fist out of his pocket and handed me some of the seeds which he normally fed Lisette. I took them with a mumbled thanks before shoving them into my mouth and instantly regretting it. They tasted bitter and cracked under my teeth, making the process of chewing and swallowing them a challenge.

Lisette gave a sharp chirp and fluttered out of his pocket to lead the way, darting from shrub to shrub along the path, snapping at the rare insect that strayed too near. From time to time, she'd return to Keely's padded shoulder before swooping away again. It was almost as if she knew that we had to move with haste, leaving the mountains behind us.

The track we were following began to lead us steeply downhill, forcing us to go slower than I would have liked, and I saw the valley stretching out below us, a grand vista of green and patches of white. A forest of pines waved at us in the wind, and from this vantage point we could see a cluster of buildings on the other side of the trees and a wisp of smoke rising above the sea of green.

'It should take at least a day to get there,' Keely commented. I could feel his displeasure, which radiated off him in waves, all because we wouldn't get supplies before reaching the town.

'Do you know how to hunt or set snares?' I asked hopefully, privately wishing that my stomach would stop complaining about its lack of sustenance all day. To ease my head, which was starting to spin, I reached for my water flask and drank.

'No,' Keely replied, 'never really had a reason to learn how.' I felt my heart sink in disappointment; would we be able to scrounge together some kind of repast today? Or would we have to wait until we reached the distant town?

Dolce had reached the bottom of the slope and stepped carefully over an icy creek bed, before treading forward through the heather, towards the first wave of trees. Down here the wind was less strong than it had been before, but the piercing cold remained, and I wriggled my toes and pushed my hands into the folds of my cloak. I didn't want to run the risk of getting frostbite. Maybe at the next town I might find some proper fur boots or gloves, but I'd need more money for that. Damn Mrs Jenkins for paying less than she ought! Those meagre few coppers I had would barely afford to buy enough supplies to see us reach the end of the Eastern Way, let alone afford passage across the Meridian.

'No matter though,' Keely said, 'it can't be that hard to catch a rabbit.'

It turned out to be much harder than he had imagined. By the time we had reached a small clearing that we deemed a safe distance from the Lightbringer Mountains, it was late afternoon. Already the sun was setting, and I sent Keely off into the undergrowth to find something to eat. My stomach was churning from lack of food and sleep and I clutched my cloak tighter around my shivering body as I tried to make a small fire. Dolce and Nancy were enjoying the end of our journey for the day and made themselves comfortable grazing. Not far from the clearing there was a thin stream that wound its way in and out of the closely packed trees.

As night drew closer, my cold fingers fumbled clumsily with the flint and tinder, and I cursed aloud as, no matter how hard I tried, no spark was able to light the kindling. I felt tears prick behind my eyes and desperately fought against them. The last thing I wanted was for Keely to see me crying.

He had been gone for a while, and I was on the point of giving up when he returned, a small creature over his shoulder.

'Need some help?' he asked casually, and I nodded. To my annoyance, he succeeded where I had failed, and it only took him three attempts to get a flame. I sat back against a tree and silently fumed at his easy ability to light a fire. His coarse hands placed the flint down next to my foot and he withdrew a knife from his belt and began to skin the rabbit.

Slowly I bent down and retrieved the flint before placing some more sticks onto the flames. The wood was quickly devoured and the fire rose higher, desperate for more. I obliged and continued to feed it until Keely had finished preparing the meat. He speared the dripping meat and held it over the flames, rotating it slowly.

'I'm afraid I don't know how to make a spit,' I said softly.

'It's alright,' Keely replied, 'but we're going to be here a while waiting for this to cook. One often gets lonesome when there isn't much to say, but I've found that telling the odd tale will liven even the heaviest of hearts.'

I watched him closely, wondering what he was aiming at. There seemed to be something he was hiding; something didn't make sense.

'How often have you been sitting around campfires to hear these tales?' I asked, 'I thought you lived in Little Fleming.'

Keely smiled to himself and continued to turn the blade.

'It doesn't matter how I know,' he said and instantly my guard was up. My body tensed for instant flight and my hand reached down to grasp my dagger. 'I'm not a Tracker,' he said smoothly, and Lisette chirped loudly, as if in agreement. 'But there is someone I'd like us to meet before we head east.'

'Who?' I tried to keep my voice steady.

'My sister,' he said placidly, 'I need to make sure she's prepared for the oncoming spring. She works on a farm by herself you know, and winter is often the hardest time for her.'

'I didn't know you had a sister,' I said. My eyes never left his face, gazing intently into his eyes to see him falter, twitch or a flicker of something, *anything* that would tell me he was lying. But his breathing didn't appear to change and nor did his expression as he said quietly,

'There's a lot about me you don't know, milady.'

Chapter Six

I didn't know what to say. Panic and fear were coursing through my veins and yet there was a sense of calm about him that just filled my mind with ease.

'I can't trust you,' I said harshly, 'you must understand that.'

He flinched as if I'd punched him. 'You don't trust me yet.' He corrected me.

My eyes widened in confusion and I felt myself slump down. My muscles were crying out plaintively, complaining at being held tense for so long.

'I never lied to you,' Keely continued slowly, 'I don't want any harm to come to you, milady. It's important that you reach safety and avoid the Usurper's minions.'

A dry and empty laugh escaped me. The idea was ridiculous. Safety? Me? Bad luck followed me everywhere. It had become a fact of life after my seventh birthday. After … no, I couldn't reminisce down memory lane now.

'You don't know much about me, Keely,' I finally said, 'anyone who has tried to help me has failed. There is no safe place for me in Scardia, and once he knows that you're with me, the Usurper will send his dogs to hunt you down. There's no escaping them.'

'There *is*,' he insisted, 'the east. The Winter Spirit said it herself: you must return to your mother's homeland.'

Slowly I relinquished my grip on my dagger and relaxed again, why, I did not know. Perhaps there was something about his odd conviction which encouraged me to trust him.

'You said you was going to tell me the story about the Winter Spirit,' Keely said.

'*Were*,' I muttered, 'when did I say that?'

'Earlier,' Keely reminded, 'you said she was called the Ice Queen.'

'Right,' I said slowly, 'the Ice Queen.'

Keely edged forward slightly and began cutting up the roasted meat. My stomach grumbled loudly and my mouth watered at the smell. As he placed the meat onto a piece of bark, I snatched it out of his hands and began to devour it. It didn't bother me that the inside was still bloody and slightly raw because it was beginning to fill the empty hole in my stomach.

He was still watching me closely and I realised that he was expecting me to tell him the story. I swallowed the last morsel of meat and felt a pang as I looked at my empty plate of bark. Keely began his own meal and I stared at his small pile of meat enviously. Perhaps the only way to distract myself would be to tell him the tale.

'She wasn't always called the Ice Queen,' I began, 'her name was Deidre. She was born back in the early dawning of Time, when Erthor, King of the Moon and Fionne, Queen of the Spring, wed. Theirs was a happy union, albeit sometimes a difficult one. Together they had three children. The eldest, Esmerelda, had long blonde hair and dancing green eyes with a bubbling laugh. Due to her dazzling appearance, Esmerelda was named the Summer Princess.

'The second child to Erthor and Fionne was a tall boy. He took after his father in both looks and personality. His parents called him Richard, Prince of the Stars.

'However, the third child of the king and queen took after neither. She was taller than average, with long white hair and clear, striking eyes, like ice. She was named Deirdre after her grandmother.

'From an early age, Deidre was shunned by other children who preferred her sister's sunny nature or her brother's quiet discussions. Other children may have run to their mothers to cry at the way other children treated them, but yet again, Deidre was different. She knew that her mother and father felt no special love for her, anyone could tell that each separate parent had their favourite child. Unbeknownst to her parents or siblings however, Deidre discovered that she had power over the elements of winter. Snow and frost would appear at her command, and she amused herself with creating small whirling snowstorms and intricate icicles. One day she was discovered by her sister and, terrified of the consequences of concealing her powers, Deidre fled.

'She spirited herself away in a snowstorm and no one heard of her again. She was content in her solitude and began to relish her control over the wintry weather. She created a palace of snow and ice which was hidden from view by a constant snowstorm. Deidre was determined to never again be at people's mercy as she had been in her parents' home.

'The years passed and the local village began to circulate stories of the Ice Queen, who lived in her fearsome palace and relished bringing winter early to the valley. One day a traveller arrived and was convinced by the townspeople to lure the mysterious woman to the village where she would be killed.'

Keely choked for a moment, then said, 'why did they want to kill her?'

'They believed her death would stop the almost eternal winter,' I shrugged, 'they weren't clever enough to realise that they lived so far north that it wouldn't change a thing.

'Anyway, the traveller was told he would be paid handsomely for his efforts and so he set out to find the palace. By now his curiosity was strong and he fought his way through the snowstorms with a vengeance. Eventually he reached the palace, never before had he seen such splendidly cut ice, which spiralled into towers and high arches. He stood in awe before knocking on the front door. It was made of thick blocks of ice which pulled away from his touch and allowed him inside. As he stepped over the threshold the door reformed behind him.

'He charmed the Ice Queen and realised that her heart was not as cold nor as hardened as he had been led to believe. For many days he stayed in her palace, slowly convincing her that the village would be honoured by her visit and not reviled. The promise of gold and silver ruled him, and the Ice Queen gradually began to believe herself in love with him. No one had ever been interested in her before nor had they accepted her abilities. Over the course of a week the traveller had promised her that she had his heart, and she had agreed to return with him to the village.

'The village seemed deserted when they arrived but as they entered the inn, the Ice Queen was ambushed and tied up. She watched, horrified, as the traveller to whom she had pledged all, was given gold and left. The townspeople left her in a locked room and began arguing over how best to kill her.

'In her room the Ice Queen's heart hardened and she urged the elements of winter to come to her aid. Once again, she was saved by a snowstorm. The townspeople heard the commotion and realised what had happened. Frenzied, they grabbed their weapons and followed her trail, determined to finish her once and for all.

'The traveller began to feel ashamed of his actions and saw the villagers' torches. He followed them to the palace and slipped through a side entrance to warn the Ice Queen. Instead of being pleased to see him, she was furious and believed that he had led the villagers to her refuge. He pleaded and apologised to no avail. It wasn't until he reminded her of his love- which he claimed to now be true- did she falter.'

'It seems like he changes his mind quickly,' Keely snorted, 'why did she forgive him when she could have turned him into an icicle?' I bit back a smile at his indignation.

'It's a story, Keely. I don't know why they reconciled, only that they did. There was no way they could escape from the villagers who had begun to rampage through the castle, torching everything in sight. The walls were melting around them and the ceiling was starting to collapse. Together they stood on the windowsill and the Ice Queen pointed out the northern lights. Their bodies were found by the villagers the next day, piled underneath ice and snow. And yet the tale goes that their spirits stepped out when they did, and instead of falling down, travelled upwards and joined the northern lights.'

Keely had his chin resting on his hand and Lisette was perched on his knee, her head turned to one side as though she too had been listening as my story drew to its close.

'She became the Winter Spirit after that,' I said.

Keely was silent as I took a swig of water from my flask. An aching tiredness was seeping through my bones, sapping my strength with painful ease. Above us the moon was climbing through the sky, its piercing rays slightly hidden by the dark leaves.

'It's sad,' Keely said quietly.

I shrugged and lay back with my pack propped under my head for a makeshift pillow.

'It's just a story, Keely,' I muttered sleepily as my eyes slid shut. A small part of me resisted the urge to sleep, protesting that our fire must surely be visible for any nearby Trackers. But the Lord of Spring had been very clear that he would give us two days to escape. Surely he would have warned me if there had been Trackers coming from the other direction, wouldn't he? Before I could wonder about it anymore, sleep overtook me.

I awoke with aching muscles and stretched. My thighs were stiff with cold and I massaged life back into them, gritting my teeth as pain rushed through my body. Keely gave a low rumbling snore from the other side of the extinguished fire. I sighed and threw a pile of soggy pine needles onto his face.

Lisette squawked indignantly and ruffled her feathers, as Keely murmured something incomprehensible and rolled over. I rose to my feet with a slight wobble and clutched onto a nearby branch for support. The wood was cold, and wet sludge oozed between my fingers as I clung tighter. I wrinkled my nose in distaste and let go, rubbing my hands along my skirt, leaving behind muddy trails.

'Come on, Keely,' I said, and was met by a low grumbling moan. Dolce snorted and a puff of steam hovered around her mouth. I stroked her neck and pressed my forehead into her mane, breathing in the scent of pine and musty fur. Behind me, I heard Keely slowly getting to his feet and kicking slushy snow over the remains of last night's fire. Without looking at him, I pulled myself up into the saddle and gazed at the forest around us. There was no way of telling which way we should continue, for in the early dawn I could barely distinguish the path we had taken the night before.

'This way, milady,' Keely said, and I mutely followed him through the trees. The morning air bit and tugged at my clothes and I pulled my cloak closer. Ahead of me, Keely urged Nancy into a brisk trot and I copied him, until the trees were growing thinner around us and we could see open plains ahead.

'The town's ahead,' Keely called, and I followed his pointing hand towards the far end of the plains. Sure enough, smoke rose into the sky from various chimneys, and the dark silhouettes of houses were dotting the horizon. As we drew closer, I saw farmers tending their fields, which were speckled with sheep.

'Let's avoid it,' I said quickly, 'we can't run the risk of being caught by Trackers.'

'And if we *do* avoid it, the townspeople will notice us even more,' Keely replied, 'there's nowhere to hide and skirt around it. They've probably already seen us coming and will expect us to pass through. Besides,' he added, 'it'll be good to stop for a proper meal and get some supplies.'

This idea didn't bode all too well with me, but I kept my mouth shut. There was no Tracker Tower in this town, nor one nearby, so if he was to turn me in it wouldn't be here. Besides, I wanted to trust Keely. I hadn't felt close enough to anyone to trust them for a long time.

But it was unwise to trust people, no matter whom.

And so, it was with a suspicious frame of mind that I allowed Keely to lead me towards the town, meeting with the sparse track and following it. As we passed fields, the farmers paused for a moment, raising their eyes to examine the newcomers. On the edge of some of the fields were darkened ruins of past houses, which were still blackened with soot. A chill went through me and I peered closer, noticing the symbol etched into the stonework.

The imprinted shadow of a bull's head. The mark of the Usurper.

This town had known the Usurper's displeasure, that much was evident, perhaps for harbouring fugitives or members of the Resistance. Who knew how they would react if they knew that the lost princess was entering their midst. Would they willingly protect me? Or hand me over to the man who had already shown how he punished those who defied him?

I stiffened my back and kept my eyes on Keely's back until we were entering the town and dismounting before the inn. I didn't want to glance back, to see the gibbets lining the main road, their long dead occupants curled up in the cages. The price this village had paid was constantly there, reminding them of this disloyalty.

Keely gave a boy several copper coins to stable our horses and opened the door. When he saw that I wasn't following him, he reached back and grasped my elbow, pulling me behind him. The inn was crowded and loud, and no one seemed to notice two strangers entering. As we approached the bar Keely leaned down and whispered in my ear,

'Let me do the talking, Karliah.' Before I could reply he was smiling at the tired-looking barmaid and handing over some coins to pay for our lunch. My stomach was scarcely staying silent, and the sight of townspeople bending low over their plates of food was almost too much to bear. Keely led me over to a table in the corner of the room, which was half shrouded in shadows. To my surprise there was a figure sitting on one of the benches, and I instantly tried to pull away from Keely's grip, but he only held me tighter.

'It's alright,' he murmured.

My mouth was dry with fear, and questions about who the stranger was kept flitting through my mind. The figure shifted and I realised that it was a woman, instantly I felt relieved. It was clear under the Usurper's rule that women could neither become Trackers nor fight amongst his army's ranks.

As I sat cautiously down, I watched her, watching me. She wore a long, dark, hooded cloak and her face was covered except for a slit from which her eyes glinted. Her hands were hidden beneath dark fur gloves and they lay folded on the oaken table between us.

'Keely,' she said, and I was surprised at the low and slightly scratched timbre of her voice. 'I was expecting you earlier.'

'I'm sorry,' my companion replied, 'I overslept again.'

'Not an uncommon occurrence,' she said, and he grinned. 'Is this the girl you told me so much about?' She pointed to me with a wave of the hand and I froze.

Keely's arm moved around my shoulder and I flinched away, confused. What did he think he was doing?

'This is Karliah,' he said, and then paused as the innkeeper brought over two bowls of broth with thick slices of bread. As soon as the food was in front of me I couldn't refrain from hiding my famine a moment longer. I was oblivious to the slightly aloof look the stranger was giving me as I spooned up the soup as fast as was humanly possible. Too hungry to even note the burning sensation in my mouth or taste the vegetables in it, I dunked the bread and mopped up the remnants in the bowl.

It wasn't just me who was thoroughly enjoying lunch, Keely was equally, if not more, eager to have proper, nourishing food. Lisette was nibbling on breadcrumbs by his bowl, which, of course, he had crumbled before starting to eat himself. The woman watched both of us and as I wiped my mouth, I began to feel awkward again.

'So, you two are engaged,' she said, and Keely nodded, squeezing my hand with his bear-sized one. I coughed and opened my mouth to splutter a refusal, but her gaze locked onto mine. Slowly, I closed my mouth and inclined my head slightly, my gaze never leaving hers. My confusion was mounting by the second, but it didn't seem like now was the right time to ask questions, so I played along.

'It took so long to get her to agree,' Keely laughed and Lisette chirped in agreement. A few heads turned from several other diners across the room and I plastered a smile onto my face.

'I can imagine,' she said, and I felt the smile slip away at the intensity of her voice. She turned to me, 'my brother speaks highly of you, Karliah. He told me you were one of a kind.' Her eyes perused me, from my covered hair to my rough leather shoes, and I felt my unease mount. I now remembered Keely had mentioned needing to see his sister, but that did nothing to ease my tension.

'I'm sorry,' I said, forcing the words to remain calm when inside I was wound as tight as a spring, 'but I still don't know your name.'

She laughed and the sound was muffled from behind her covered mouth and nose. 'Forgive me, I was under the impression that Keely had already told you. I'm Isabel, Keely's sister.' A prickling sensation filled me, and I was certain that her name was no more Isabel than mine was Karliah.

'Where were you going to hold the wedding, Keely?' In an instant her attention was riveted back on her brother, and I felt a wave of relief wash through me.

'I wanted to get married in the west, where we grew up.' Isabel nodded in agreement. 'But Karliah wishes to go east, to wed on the other side of the Eastern Sea and remain there for the honeymoon.'

Even though her face was in shadow, I could sense her eyebrows rising in astonishment. There was an awkward silence as Isabel processed the news. Finally, she gave a strangled sort of laugh which she obviously though was light-hearted.

'You're planning on crossing the Eastern Sea to get married? Surely you don't need to go in search of any more magic.'

Keely laughed raucously and I somehow managed a smile that hopefully wasn't too pained. 'But in all seriousness,' Isabel leaned forward, 'crossing the Eastern Sea would be folly at this time of year and the lands on the other side of the Eastern Sea are just as dangerous as the crossing would be. It would be far better for you to come west and wed there.'

'That is what I tried to say,' Keely smiled, and held my rather floppy hand in his, 'but Karliah insisted. She heard tales about it from her grandmother when she was a child, you see, and...' I didn't hear anything of what he said next for my attention was fixed on the group of men who had just entered the inn. Like Isabel, their faces were masked, but that was where their resemblance ended. Their armour shimmered in the lamplight and almost instantly the inn was silenced. My hands were sweating and I could feel myself trembling, barely able to breathe through the steely grip of fear that was encircling my throat.

Dark eyes met mine and flicked away before resting on the Innkeeper. Luckily, the blades that hung at the newcomers' sides remained sheathed.

'Sustenance,' the man said in a gruff voice, 'now.'

With a low murmur of something incomprehensible, the Innkeeper obliged, hastening to pour them tankards of ale. Slowly normality resumed and conversations restarted, although they were considerably muted, with people casting surreptitious, fearful glances at the men at the bar.

'Anyway,' Isabel continued, as if nothing had happened, 'the Eastern Sea. Are you quite sure you will be prepared to go there?'

'We thought it would be romantic,' I croaked, turning to Keely beside me. Isabel's eyes widened slightly as I kissed my so-called fiancé's cheek. Keely grinned smugly.

'We'll be leaving soon,' he said, 'the wedding is set for the day after next. Then it's off across the sea.'

'Where will the ceremony take place?' Isabel asked.

'Nuuk,' Keely ruffled Lisette's feathers with his forefinger. 'Karliah would like her grandmother to see us wed.'

I had never known either grandmother. A pang pierced my heart as I realised that all the family I had was long dead, and when time did come for me to wed, I would be entirely alone.

Keely stood up, pulling me with him.

'We should be off, Isabel,' he grunted, 'long journey ahead.'

'May the Gods be with you,' Isabel replied, 'and take care. The roads from here to Nuuk can be dangerous for the unwary.'

Chapter Seven

'Who was she?' I asked Keely as soon as we were back on the road, leaving the town. He remained silent, as he had for the last hour, while we had replenished our meagre supplies. Now that we were out of earshot of any passing farmer, I felt confident enough to voice some of the many questions which were rising like a turbulent sea within me.

'Who was she, Keely?' I repeated, 'and don't try telling me that she's your sister. You don't resemble each other in the slightest.' I don't quite know how my understanding of that would be accurate considering that I hadn't seen Isabel properly, yet my intuition was screaming at me that I was right.

'You need not concern yourself with it,' he muttered, so quietly that I had to lean sideways to hear him. 'She is a friend. She wants to help.' He paused for a moment, as if weighing up how much to tell me at once, 'and she knows who you are.'

Of all things, I hadn't been expecting this. My stomach plummeted and I felt the lunch that I had eaten so quickly begin to churn around and around. At this rate half of Scardia would know my identity by the first day of summer. It was only a matter of time before the news reached the Usurper's ears, and then his Trackers would increase their searches and no one would be able to stand in their way.

'Why won't you tell me?' I persisted. This secret that he was withholding only made me trust him less and wish to leave at the next available opportunity. It didn't help my nerves that the Tracker party had arrived in the town so shortly after us. Keely remained silent, and I continued doggedly.

'Isabel didn't like that we were heading east,' I commented. 'Especially when you said that we were going across the Eastern Sea.'

My companion's mouth was a thin line. 'I know,' he said, 'I think we should go west, like she suggested.'

'But the spirit gave me clear instructions,' I whispered, 'you heard her as well as I did, Keely. And you agreed with it. We can't deny an ancient force like that.'

'I remember what I said, but I still believe that we should go west,' Keely insisted mulishly, and I threw up my hands in exasperation.

'Keely, tell me the truth. Please.'

'It won't do you no good.'

'Keely,' I took a deep breath, 'I command it. Tell me the truth.'

For the first time in years I felt like a princess again: giving orders, expecting them to be obeyed, maintaining a commanding presence. I waited expectantly, yet Keely kept his mouth firmly closed and his gaze averted. Grinding my teeth in annoyance, I turned away as well and urged Dolce forward. The silence stretched out between us and all I could hear was the sound of distant birds and the steady beating of our horses' hooves. The biting wind cut my cheek and teased strands of hair from my scarf, threatening to unveil my true identity.

'It shouldn't be too far to the coast from here,' I said finally, 'only a day's ride or so. How will we convince a captain to take us across the Meridian?'

Keely grunted something unintelligible and I bit back a sharp response. Lisette let out a loud chirp and fluttered on Keely's shoulder. I closed my eyes for a moment, trying to imagine how it would be when we arrived at Nuuk and how we could convince someone to ferry us across the Eastern Sea. Lisette screeched again and I shot a glare in her direction.

'Can't you shut that bird up, Keely?' I snapped, 'it's hard enough to try to plan how to reach the Eastern Lands when I have to do it alone, and with that budgerigar squawking all the time it's nigh on impossible.'

The bundle of green and yellow feathers launched itself at my face and beat me with her wings before landing on my shoulder and screeching in my ear. I growled and beat her away, but as I did so I noticed the shadow on the horizon following us.

'Keely,' I whispered, and my voice had lost all its irritation, all that remained was a tremble of fear. 'Keely, they're behind us.'

He turned in the saddle and his eyes widened.

'Do you think … they're the ones who … the inn?' I could barely form a coherent sentence, I was trembling so much. Keely said nothing, he just nodded. Wordlessly we urged Nancy and Dolce onwards, fleeing the line of Trackers on the horizon behind us.

I don't know if he was trying to make me feel better or just to distract me from the thoughts of capture which were running rampant throughout my head, but Keely began to speak.

'The way I see it, milady, you want answers to difficult questions, and I ain't got all the answers. I can do my best to let you know some things and I'll reply truthfully, but there's a catch.'

My guard was instantly up, battling with my raging curiosity. 'What's the catch?'

'I get the right to ask you a question for each one that you ask me. And you have to answer truthfully.'

I almost wanted to tell him to forget it. Who knew what he would want to know, and Gods knew there was so much that I wasn't prepared to tell. Not to him, not to anyone.

But there were things I wanted to know, suspicions I had to confirm, and there was only one way to find out.

'Fine.' The word tasted like ash in my mouth, and I regretted it almost as soon as I'd spoken.

'Very well,' Keely said, with a small smile. 'You wanted to know who that woman was. Whether she was my sister or not. Why she wants us to go west.'

I waited with bated breath, barely able to even nod.

'Her name's Rakael. She's no more my sister than you are. And she works for a group of people who've been looking for you for a damn long time, milady.'

'Who?'

He laughed, 'Even if I wanted to answer that I wouldn't, partly because I think you already know and also because it's my turn to ask some questions and get some answers.'

An invisible knife twisted in my stomach, and I let out a strangled, 'alright.'

'Why Karliah?'

I sat there frozen for a few moments and then said, 'Excuse me?'

'Why did you choose the name Karliah?'

While this wasn't as hard to answer as some other questions might've been, it didn't mean I really wanted to explain my name choice.

'When I was younger I read a lot,' I began, 'I wasn't allowed outside the palace grounds very often and there was only so much to do. I read almost every book in our library, but my favourites were tales of adventure or folklore.' It felt strange to share this with anyone; I'd never opened up this much before and it made me feel scarily vulnerable. 'Ever since the Dark Time I have changed my name frequently to reflect the characters I once loved so much. Karliah was a warrior queen who fought bravely and vanquished countless foes to maintain peace in her kingdom. She was a particular favourite.'

'Which is why you've been using it for so long?'

I nodded.

'What other names have you used?'

I let out a sigh, 'countless ones. I was a Brunhilda for a time, then Natasha. Sometimes I was Giselle or Nathalia. Once I was even called Clarisse, but that didn't last long. They never did. I only did what I thought necessary and would safely set me apart from any connection with the royal family.'

'And what name would you use next, after Karliah?' His tone was so cajoling and casual that my guard instantly rose. I'd revealed too much.

'That's four questions,' I said, forcing myself to keep my voice calm, 'you only answered three of mine.'

'Right,' he said, 'forgive me milady. All I wanted was for you to trust me, for you to learn to talk about the past.'

I kept my face closed and blank as I stared at the road ahead of us, barely noticing the setting sun and all too aware of his gaze. Instead, I allowed myself to consider what my next pseudonym might be, although there was no way in all of Scardia that I would let Keely know. The problem was that I was so attached to my current name that I couldn't bear to consider changing it, no matter how risky it was. The Trackers would be looking for a barmaid called Karliah from Little Fleming, so it would surely be wise to change it sooner rather than later.

'We should make camp soon,' Keely said, and I jumped as I snapped out of my thoughts.

'Do you think it's safe?' I asked warily, the image of the Trackers hovering on the edge of my mind.

'The horses need rest,' he replied, and I grudgingly agreed. We halted in a clearing a short way off from the main road and Keely withdrew his usual bag of seeds. Silently wishing we could light a fire and cook something instead of eating a handful of seeds and some dried meat, I sat down on a mossy boulder. By now the sun had almost disappeared on the horizon, and all that remained were faint traces of red and pink across the sky. Keely busied himself with the horses for several minutes and then joined me. His bulking presence made me uneasy, and I edged away slightly on the boulder. My movement did not go unnoticed, but he didn't say anything, just fed Lisette from a small pile of seeds in his hand.

Conflicting thoughts raged through my mind and I couldn't bring myself to look at my companion. The fear of being caught by Trackers had haunted me for almost as long as I could remember, ever since the Dark Times when I'd lost everything I'd believed in; stability, family, trust. There was no way that Keely could ever understand how hard it was to open up to anyone when all it led to was death and pain. He hadn't had to see what happened to those few people who, over the years, had attempted to protect and shelter me. He didn't know what the Trackers had done to them, what they'd made them suffer in the hopes of locating me. He wasn't aware of what some people had given up and lost for their princess.

'It's not bad to open up to people, milady,' Keely said quietly, and I bit my tongue to stop my retort. 'It's something you need to learn to do, to be able to confront those demons that keep you from taking your rightful place as queen.'

'Don't talk to me about that Keely.' My voice was shaky with emotion, and I got up and began to pace the clearing, trying fruitlessly to clear my head and calm down.

'Your parents wouldn't have wanted you to be living in fear as a barmaid, changing her name whenever she saw fit. They wouldn't want you to be constantly hiding from your birthright.'

'Shut your mouth.' The words were out before I could take them back, and at this point I was too angry to hold back. In that moment all the fear, suspicion and rage that I'd pent up inside me was unleashed and I couldn't stop myself. 'How would a commoner know what my parents would have wanted? As you're aware, I *have* to hide or else I'd join my parents in the afterlife. How can I be sure what they would have wanted for me? They were never here to guide me, never here to counsel me for these past years? Do you think it's *easy* to constantly run, to act as someone who supports the man who murdered my parents in cold blood? You have no idea what it's like to hear people praise him, to serve the Trackers who are in his employ. What would a man who can barely form a coherent sentence and whose closest companion is a bird know about the matters of state, the affairs of the royal family? For all I know you could be in the Usurper's employ, trying to make me feel safe, convincing me to tell you private things about myself to gain my trust.' I let out a hollow, maniacal laugh and stared at Keely's frozen expression. 'Trust only leads to pain. The last person I trusted enough to tell my name lost first their fingers, then their ears and then their eyes. That's when they started to call out for me, their princess, and our Gods, to spare them any more pain.' Keely's horrified eyes followed my pacing figure, through the twilight. 'And do you think the torturer stopped there? Of course not; for him and the others the fun had begun. It was at least five more hours before their victim breathed his last. Yet another death brought about because of me.' The bitterness was rising in my throat and tears burned my eyes as I remembered the scene, hours after my friends had been killed, finding their remains.

'Princess Nina—' Keely began but I cut him off with a wave of my hand.

'Don't talk to me,' I hissed, 'you have no right to bring up the subject of my parents nor the right to tell me what I should and shouldn't do. You have no—'

The sound of distant voices made me halt my tangent and I stood there, as frozen as Keely had been mere moments before. The anger slowly drained out of me, only to be replaced by a sensation that I knew only too well: being trapped.

'Go,' Keely muttered, ignoring my immediate protest. What I'd said still hung in the air between us, but despite my earlier words of hurt and anger, I couldn't leave him now, not with Trackers closing in. Not when it was probably the sound of my angry voice that had led them right to us.

'Nina,' he said, 'I'll be okay. I can cope.'

'No one can cope with torture,' I hissed back, gripping his hand with both of my own. 'I can't leave you, Keely, not after what I just—'

'It don't matter,' he retorted, 'you need to go.'

'I don't want you to get hurt,' I whispered, 'I wish you hadn't followed me from Little Fleming, you'd be safer if you didn't know me.'

'But then you'd be here all by yourself,' he said quietly. The sounds of horses were getting closer by the minute. 'When you have the chance to go west milady, join the rebels there. They'll be able to protect you better than I can. But first go to the docks and get on the first ship that will take you where you need to go. There's an inn – the Seven Wastrels, a man might be able to help you there.'

Tears were pooling in my eyes and yet I clung tighter to his hand as the sounds of men's voices grew gradually closer.

'I'm sorry,' I whispered. 'I'm so sorry.'

Keely shook his head impatiently, 'they know I'm with you, Nina. Go now and I'll distract them. Here,' he took a bundle of quivering feathers out of his pocket, 'take Lisette. She'll look after you.'

Lisette gave a low chirrup and nipped his finger before fluttering onto my shoulder.

'Go now!' Keely hissed and pushed me towards Dolce. With one last look at his weather-beaten face, I obeyed.

Chapter Eight

I didn't look back as I rode silently through the trees and tried to block my ears to the sounds coming from the clearing behind me. Yet even so, the distant cries and sound of blows struck at my heart with a bitter pain. Tears slid down my cheeks and I rubbed them away with a rough jerk of the back of my hand.

There was no point in being emotional now, I had to move on, keep ahead of my pursuers. Besides, who knew how long Keely would hold out before the Trackers had enough and left his corpse in the damp grass? My breath caught in my throat at the thought, and I took a shuddering breath. There was nothing I could do now except continue on the path set out for me by the Winter Spirit. She had said to cross the Meridian to the Eastern Lands from whence my mother had come, and so to the Eastern Lands I would go.

In the darkness, the moonlight cast long shadows on the ground and I flinched at every movement, certain that with each second my capture was drawing closer. My fingers hovered over my knife which I drew out of its sheath and held in my lap. Lisette ruffled her feathers on my shoulder and nipped my ear, in what I hoped was an affectionate manner.

'I'm worried about him too, Lisette,' I murmured. 'I wish I hadn't said what I did.'

She squawked in agreement and edged closer to my ear, before letting out a series of quick, soft chirps. I could almost imagine her saying, 'do something that would make Keely happy: tell a story.'

And so I began a story that I had been told since the days before I could remember, a tale that was one of the closest to my heart and I hoped that, by speaking it aloud in a mere whisper, Keely would be able to hear it and gain strength from it.

'It all began a long, long time ago,' I began, my breath leaving a light fog in its wake as I started my tale. 'Once upon a time there were two kingdoms separated by a stretch of water that held many names: The Meridian, the Eastern Sea and the Separator between the Uncanny and the Sane. For many years, war had raged between the two kingdoms, until one day when the king of Scardia decided to make peace.

'He entered negotiations with the king of the Eastern Lands, and the answer to the war seemed simple: marriage. Luckily the king had a son, and the Eastern Lands was rumoured to have a princess of indescribable beauty and grace. And so, after many months of ships relaying back and forth messages, a date was agreed upon when the prince and princess would meet for the first time. The king of Scardia took his son Vincent to the East- a land of magic and mystery and home of Elvenkind, sorcerers and healers.

'On his arrival, Vincent was astounded by the world around him. He gazed around in wonder, for the Elves lived in harmony with the world around them. Giant trees, untouched by axe or saw, rose towards the celestial heavens above. The Elven ambassador who greeted them wore robes made up of the finest silk, embedded with feathers and leaf skeletons. He had sharp features with pale blue eyes, and as he bowed to the Scardians, Vincent noticed how his ears rose to fine points. He'd anticipated this, thanks to the many tales he had been told as a boy.

'With a silent gesture, the ambassador beckoned them to follow him up a twisting staircase made up of woven ivy and willow branches. Vincent barely noticed the leaves and twigs that clung to his clothing or the way his cloak snagged on the twisting snakes of ivy. He didn't notice the ground drawing further and further away as they drew closer to the zenith of the trees. Tiny, winged creatures fluttered around his head, hovering for brief moments so that he could catch a glance of mischievous eyes, a flash of colour or pointed pale faces. He blinked and the creatures became a mere blur, and he was left to wonder if what he'd seen had been real or imaginary.

'The soft sound of reed flutes and a light drumbeat greeted the visitors as they finished climbing. The ambassador smiled at the other courtiers, who stood around the edges of a large platform, eyeing the newcomers. Self-consciously, Vincent brushed away the leaf litter which clung to him and silently envied the ambassador who, unlike the Scardians, hadn't even broken into a sweat during the climb.

'Once he had caught his breath, Vincent looked around and saw that the platform they were standing on was connected to others on different trees by interwoven bridges of vines and willow. On most platforms were houses with conical roofs, their walls made of pale, woven birch. The doorways were different from the solid, bolted oak doors in Scardia, for here they were made up of strings of shells, feathers or leaves. The faint murmurs from the Elves around them fell to a hushed silence as a tall blond Elf emerged from a doorway of oak leaves. He looked proud and haughty, and there was a glint in his eyes which Vincent didn't like. His gossamer robes whispered around his feet and a woven circlet of holly adorned his head.

'Vincent's father stepped forward and placed two fingers on his forehead and bowed respectfully, his entourage following suit. The Elven king smiled and copied the gesture before sitting down on what Vincent assumed was a throne. It was a rough wooden chair with engravings of leaves and various creatures, and the back rose in three sharp points towards the sky.

"King Leopold,' his voice was silvery and low, like a spring breeze, 'we bid you welcome to our lands, and we hope that your stay enables us to overcome the differences of the past to achieve a brighter future.'

"Thank you, King Aegis,' Vincent's father replied, 'may I present my son, Vincent?'

'With a subtle push from one of his retainers, Vincent stumbled forward. He bowed to King Aegis and stammered through a formal introduction. His ears were going red with embarrassment; almost capturing the same colour as his hair, save for its streak of white.

"I'm afraid my daughter is out of sorts,' King Aegis said, 'but she will be present for tonight's meal. My ambassador will show you to your quarters.'

'Their quarters were inside one of the birch houses, which spanned up and down the trunk of the tree, branching out from the trunk itself. Magic must prevent these houses from toppling to the ground below, Vincent thought, for no ordinary tree could cope with being so top-heavy.

'Dusk fell and they were led to a banqueting table, which was glistening with sweet meats, herbed breads and delicate soups. King Aegis greeted them and indicated that they should sit on either side of him.

"May I present my daughter, Lydia?' A curvy young woman with escorts on either side of her curtsied low to Vincent and his father. She sat beside Vincent and he almost gagged from the smell of rosewater. Her dark, lustrous hair was twisted high on her head and her dark eyes glistened in delight as she glanced around. Throughout the first course Vincent watched her, working up the courage to speak.

"I was sorry to hear that you were unwell earlier, I pray that you feel better now.'

She glanced at him briefly and said,"Thank you, I do feel better. In fact,' she was eyeing up one of King Leopold's retainers coyly, 'I cannot wait to dance.' The retainer blushed slightly as she smiled at him and Vincent looked away, wishing fervently that he had a brother who could marry this princess in his place.

'All of a sudden, a hint of musk assaulted his senses and with a jolt he became aware of the warm breath of a girl leaning over his shoulder, refilling his wine glass. He turned and saw her willowy figure, light strawberry blond hair and pale blue eyes. Her lips parted in an 'oh' of shock as she realised that she had captured his attention.

"Forgive me if I disturbed you, your highness,' she stammered, and he felt his heart do a small somersault. There was a delicacy about her, a quiet sophistication that the princess beside him lacked. Forgetting all senses of propriety, he grasped her arm as she made to move away.

"What is your name?'

"Celine, my lord.' Her hair sheltered her bowed head, his grip slacked and she moved away. However, for the rest of the night the humble prince of Scardia was aware, not of the princess in her resplendent finery beside him, but of the low-voiced servant girl who carried the decanter in her capable hands.

'The next three days passed slowly, each one filled with the supervised courtship of the prince and princess. In this time, Vincent became ever more certain that should he marry Lydia, he would never find true happiness. On the fourth day he escaped her presence by pleading tiredness, and instead found himself wandering the Elven village.

'He found her sitting beside one of the long staircases which meandered down to the ground. She was singing words he couldn't quite distinguish, and her strawberry blond hair rippled in the breeze as he edged closer, awestruck. She knew he was there, of that he was certain, not that she'd made any kind of acknowledgement of his presence. Only when he sat down next to her did she turn and stare at him, pale eyes grave.

'"Your highness, what brings you here?'

'Vincent could hardly speak, as though his tongue had twisted itself into a triple knot, rendering him incapable of speech. He had often been told by his father that it was un-kingly to be afraid to speak. Nervousness was for mutes or imbeciles, for a true prince need never fear anything. It was no surprise that the relationship between father and son was rocky at best. King Leopold constantly reprimanded his son, whom some said was more curse to him than blessing.

'Of course, Vincent enjoyed many of the same pursuits as a true prince ought. He could fight well and was an avid hunter. Yet he was not a fan of politics despite his father's hopes. He preferred to read novels of far-off places and dream of impossibilities instead of dealing with political reality. Another disappointment for the king was his son's appearance. Instead of being tall and dashingly handsome, he was rather short and stocky, with flaming red hair that got tangled too easily. He had always been self-conscious of the streak of white that distinguished him as the rightful heir to the throne.

'Yet now, next to this vision of perfection he could barely think, let alone speak. Finally, she realised that he was not going to say anything and turned away, serenely contemplating the world below.

"I always envied your people,' she said after a long silence, 'you were always so passionate in both war and peace. I could never understand why. But you mortals have such strong feelings; at times they blind you to what is really important. At times your people scare me.' For a moment Vincent sat in shocked silence. And then before he knew it, he was pouring out his hopes and dreams to this mystical creature of starlight and serenity. He told her about his father's constant disappointment, about his passion for riding and his wonder at the Eastern Kingdom. He shared his fears about ruling, and how he wasn't ready to wed a woman he could not hold high in his esteem. On that note he paused, worried that she would take offense for the Elven Princess.

"But surely you want to bring peace to the everlasting war between our peoples,' she said calmly. 'Marriage is the only simple way to restore the wrongs and make a right.'

"Yes,' Vincent agreed, 'I understand that, but I cannot- I *will* not - marry a woman I do not love. It matters not whether she has the fairest manners or complexion. As you can see,' he indicated himself with a wave of the hand, 'I am not the most well-endowed prince, I lack the patience for strategic meetings and the dashing charm and strapping appearance to win a fair maiden's heart.'

'Celine was silent for a while, her gaze fixed on the streak of white in his hair. He felt as though she could take in every aspect of him with that one look.

"You do not credit yourself on the parts of you that are unseen,' she said, 'your kindness and noble heart for example, or the strong loyalty you have for your country. I'm sure the princess must hold you in high esteem for those qualities.' Vincent highly doubted this but kept his opinion to himself.

'A week more passed before Vincent's father approached him about the upcoming nuptials. For the past few days, Vincent had fallen into the habit of courting Lydia in the day and meeting Celine secretly under the stars. During this time his contempt for Lydia had increased, whereas his feelings towards Celine had matured into something much more lasting. He had worked up the courage to tell his father that he could not marry Lydia, and King Leopold's response was exactly as he'd feared it would be. He stormed around his son's quarters, shouting about his son's stubbornness, his insubordination, and his unwillingness to help his country, not caring that the passing Elves could hear every word.

'Embarrassed and hurt, Vincent tried to reason with his father but to no avail. On hearing about his son's love for Celine, King Leopold spluttered,

"So you would dismiss a young lady of refinement and good birth for some paltry maid?'

"She's more than just a maid,' Vincent replied hotly, 'she's smart and beautiful and she loves me, I know it.' Even though she had said no such thing, Vincent was certain of it. All the same, King Leopold scorned his son's feelings, believing him to have been ensnared by a common serving wench. And so it was with a heavy heart the following day that Vincent stood in his wedding. Everyone was decked out in their best clothes, with the Elves outshining everyone else. Vincent's father stood next to him at the altar, his presence reminding him of his duty to his country and the upcoming betrayal of his heart.

'King Aegis stood on his other side and was watching him intently. His palms sweating, Vincent glanced between them and eventually said, "I can't do it, I can't.' His father looked at him aghast and embarrassed while King Aegis looked on calmly.

"Shut your mouth boy,' Leopold hissed, his hand rising to grip his son's neck.

"Why can't you marry my daughter, Prince of Scardia?' King Aegis asked coolly, 'does she not please you?'

"She is very pleasant my lord,' Vincent replied quickly, 'but my heart belongs to another in your hall.'

"And who would that be?'

"Celine, my lord.' Aegis' eyebrows rose.

"A maid?'

"Exactly: a maid,' Leopold intervened, 'what can a maid possibly have that a princess doesn't?'

"I love her,' Vincent said.

"Do you indeed?' Aegis asked, 'and does she return your affection?'

"I hope so,' Vincent said after a pause, 'I can hope that she feels something for me and maybe it will grow into love.'

"You would be willing to abandon your crown to be with her if the need arose? To dismiss the chance to bring peace between Elf and man: that which your father has spent so long trying to achieve?'

Aegis' words made Leopold bridle with anger.

"No son of mine is going to give away his crown for a paltry maid!'

"Yes,' Vincent replied simultaneously. Both father and son looked at each other for a long time before King Leopold looked away, disgusted. There was no point in arguing with his son, all that he had worked for to mend what his father and his father's father had set into motion would be for nothing, all thanks to his son's thoughtless decision.

"Daughter,' King Aegis called, 'come and join us.'

'Vincent felt a stab of shame in the pit of his stomach at the thought of seeing Lydia again, after publicly rejecting her. He kept his eyes on the ground, unable to meet the gaze of the woman on whom the hopes of his father and his country had been pinned. Her slippered feet were dainty as she stepped closer to him. Before he knew it, a slender hand lifted his chin, forcing his gaze upwards. Still he stubbornly kept his eyes facing downward.

"Look at me.' The voice that spoke was as soft and musical as it had been the first night he heard it. He froze in shock, realising that the voice was not the same as the woman he had known as Lydia during his visit. For a moment he couldn't believe that it was real.

"My lords,' King Aegis declared, 'I present my daughter, the Lady Lydia of the Eastern Lands.'

King Leopold was the first of the Scardians to recover.

"Now look here Aegis,' he blustered, 'what on earth were you doing by playing that sort of joke on us? It's very indecent of you; it's almost as if you *wanted* the war between us to continue.'

"Do not blame my father, my lord,' Lydia said, 'it was my choice and mine alone. My maidservant and I swapped roles so that I could determine the character of the prince. My father likes tricks and tests and was all too happy to approve of my actions.' Vincent barely noticed what she was saying, all that he registered was that she was there and was Aegis' daughter.

"I wanted to know whether he could love me if he thought I had nothing before he found out the truth.'

"You have led my son on a merry dance,' King Leopold said, 'and you're lucky he could recognise good breeding when he saw it.' Both King Aegis and his daughter exchanged a private glance. There was no point in arguing with him.

"But does she love him?' Leopold asked, 'does this mean that, for the first time in centuries, we can end this war amicably?'

"Yes,' Lydia said, smiling. King Leopold yelled in triumph and clapped his son on the shoulder to the resounding cheers of his retainers. But Vincent didn't register the cacophony around him, all he was aware of was Celine, caught up in the moment and relishing the fact that they could be together.'

My tale ended as the sun began to rise, and I could see the sea coming closer and closer. Lisette was sleeping on my shoulder, but the fresh morning air ensured that I stayed awake, still caught up in the tale. In my mind I could see the young couple, hands clasped on that great tree surrounded by courtiers, their hopes for the future so bright. And the following years were blissful; they were blessed with a daughter who would become the last and sole heir to the Ice Flame. Me.

Chapter Nine

I drank deeply from my hip flask and stretched in the saddle, before dismounting and leading Dolce on foot down the main street. The seaside township of Nuuk was a dark and foreboding place. The houses rose tall and narrow, each packed so tightly to the others that they worked together to block out what little sunlight was available. Bare trees lined the streets, looking like the skeletons of some ancient spirits from the land in a time before our own. Despite the early hour, there were already people moving around the streets, their faces pinched against the cold, unwilling to enter into conversation. I copied them, forcing my gaze downward. My target came up faster than I had imagined, and I was soon standing in front of the Seven Wastrels Inn. Keely had said that a man might be able to help me here. Perhaps he was one of those sailors who, on coming in from a long journey at sea, would head to the closest inn instead of going home to his family.

I led Dolce to the stable and noticed that her saddlebags were larger than they had been when we left. I opened them and to my astonishment saw that there was a large money bag and the remaining supplies we had bought the previous day, along with another blanket. Keely had obviously been prepared for the worst last night, which made me feel even worse about how I'd treated him.

I left Dolce to rest and entered the inn. On pushing open the door, the stale smell of spilt beer and unwashed males assaulted my nostrils. The barkeep was so busy in discussion with early morning customers that he didn't notice my entrance. Taking advantage of my invisibility, I glanced around and noticed a small head duck away behind a doorway. Intrigued, I followed the figure down a dark flight of stairs and found myself in a dirty kitchen. Pots and pans lay scattered across the floor and an oak table. And there, huddled in the corner, was a small figure.

It was a small boy, not much older than eleven or twelve summers at least. His appearance was, on the whole, shabby and maltreated, and in my mind screamed out for help, perhaps from a bath and a bar of soap.

'Hello,' I said, and he cowered away. I didn't like the way he flinched at the sound of my voice and how he instinctively curled in on himself, as if fearing a beating. 'You don't need to be afraid,' I added quickly, 'I won't hurt you.'

He glanced up at me through his scraggly hair as if to check that I was telling the truth.

'I wasn't scared,' he said defiantly, 'I'm not scared of anything.'

The lie was so obvious behind the false bravado that it was almost laughable. But I maintained a straight face as he wiped his nose on his sleeve.

'What's your name?' I asked, and was shot another furtive glance.

'Olaf,' he mumbled, 'I help Mister MacMillan with cleaning the inn. He's not my father,' he added, 'my parents died three winters ago. He took me in and said I had to earn my way like everyone else.'

'And do you … like working here?' I asked delicately.

'Not much,' he admitted, staring at the floor for a moment, 'but Mister Macmillan says I'll have more luck here than doing what I want to do.'

'And what's that?'

He kicked the floor and avoided my gaze, 'you'd laugh. All the grown-ups laugh.'

'I won't,' I said, and when he remained unconvinced, I added, 'promise.'

'Iwannabeaknight,' he said, so fast that the words blurred together and it took me several moments to figure out what he had actually said.

'You want to be a knight?' I said slowly, and he nodded. The idea of this dishevelled boy becoming a knight was highly unlikely, but then who was I to judge? 'Well, there have been worse dreams, and less noble ones. But you're never going to get closer to achieving it if you stay here. Once you start working in a place like this,' I glanced around in distaste, remembering the inn at Little Fleming, 'it becomes harder and harder to leave.'

He was looking at me now, not the dirt-stained floor, and I was slightly shocked at the astonishment in his eyes. Was it possible that I was the first person who hadn't mocked his dream? When he didn't say anything, I concluded that I must be right, and knelt down so that we were at eye-level.

'Do you have anyone else that can take care of you?' I asked, suddenly filled with a strange compassion. 'Grandparents, aunts, uncles?'

'No,' he said, and rubbed his nose on his sleeve again.

'Then why stay?' I said, 'if you want to be a knight, why stay here and scrub dishes?'

'Mister Macmillan says it's a whimsy dream for someone like me,' Olaf muttered, 'he always laughed at it and said I was good for nothing, save inn work. Besides, I haven't got any money. You can't go places if you don't have money. He says it's better if I don't even try.'

My heart was breaking at this point, partly from the recent loss of Keely and partly from seeing the result of years of abuse in front of me. Instinctively, I reached out and pulled Olaf close to me, ignoring the greasy hair and clothes. At my touch he stiffened and trembled, but when he realised that I wasn't going to hit him, he began to slowly relax. He reminded me so much of myself that it hurt.

'Would you like to leave this place, Olaf?' I asked quietly, and felt his shaky nod on my shoulder. 'Then from now on,' I told him, 'you are my brother Erik. I need someone to keep me safe and look after me and you need to have a chance to see the world and experience some new things before deciding what is and isn't possible.'

Learning how to take a proper bath would be high on the list of priorities, I added silently. Olaf smiled for the first time, and I realised that there was no going back now.

'You mean it?' He asked.

Gods save me.

'Yes,' I replied, and he clung tighter, squeezing the breath out of me. While one part of me revelled in the moment, another was berating me, screaming at me that I was stupid and thoughtless. What was I getting myself into? What had Keely's presence done to my once rigid set of rules so that now I was desperate to have company again?

Lisette chirped and I couldn't tell if it was in approval or not, but I agreed with her, this whole situation had just gotten more complicated. But then I realised that this boy could in fact be my godsend; the Trackers were looking for a teenage girl travelling alone, not a brother and sister. This could perhaps buy me some extra time in Nuuk to find a captain.

'Get your things together and meet me by the stables,' I said, rising to my feet. 'We have to get moving quickly.'

'You'll come?' He asked and I nodded. But now it was time to find a captain.

Chapter Ten

Mister Macmillan was a big, beefy man who spared no time on civilities.

'What were you doing down there?' He said, 'you've got no right going into the kitchen.'

'I wasn't aware it was the kitchen,' I replied truthfully, 'not until I was in there. I met your kitchen hand, and I think you should know that he's not staying here. Not after the way you've treated him.'

'You've got some nerve—' he began angrily, but I cut him off.

'Let's forget for a moment that you've grossly mistreated that poor boy after his parents died, and that you've let him live in a pigsty. I need to find a captain who will be able to offer me transport.'

His face was slowly turning redder and redder, and I knew it was only a matter of time before he exploded. I leaned forward and slid some coins across the counter, which disappeared in a flash as his colour started to return to normal.

'At this time of year it'd be folly to go anywhere. We've had one of Scardia's harshest winters and the ice is only just starting to melt. He'd have to be ludicrous to accept such an offer.' I withdrew some more silver and he continued, 'but come to think of it, a ship is getting ready to set sail any day now. When you go to the Western docks ask for Captain

Markus. He might be able to see you on your way. Where did you say you were heading?'

'I didn't,' I replied and left the inn quickly to avoid any more questions.

Erik could hardly believe that I'd kept my word. As asked, he had brought a satchel containing all of his belongings which, on closer perusal, turned out to be as meagre as my own. I had already decided that our first point of call before the port was the general trader. If I was to have a brother now it would be better if he didn't look like a beggar. Who knew how hard it would be to convince this Captain Markus to offer us passage? In any case he would probably be more inclined to accept aboard a respectably dressed brother and sister. 'Now Erik,' I said as we entered the shop and he picked out some clothes, 'you need to remember to respond to Erik now, not Olaf. Your name is Erik Merryweather and I'm your sister Karliah.'

'That's not really your name, is it?' He asked suddenly. I paused for a moment, and then continued as though he hadn't spoken.

'Our parents died in a forest fire last summer and we're going across the Meridian to live with our only remaining family.'

His eyes went wide, 'we're going across the Meridian?'

I smiled and nodded, 'to the land of magic and mystery.'

Who knew what we'd actually do once we *got* there, the Winter Spirit hadn't been specific, but I would figure that out later. And I couldn't deny that a part of me was pleased to cross the sea, to finally escape Scardia and the dangers within her borders. Another part longed to find my mother's family, who until now I had barely thought of, for I had never met them and never heard from them. As a child they had always been distant, sending occasional letters but never making the journey across the sea to visit.

'Cool,' Erik said. I paid the shop's owner quickly for Erik's new clothes, and ushered him out, leading him and Dolce down to the docks. The wind cut through my cloak and I shivered, clenched my jaw and pushed on through the throng of people who were yelling incoherent words, carrying bundles and laughing raucously. Masts and creaking ships stretched out before us, and the grey water chopped savagely against the dock.

'Excuse me, do you know where I could find Captain Markus?' I asked a man who was balancing three crates filled with rolls of multi-coloured cloth. He shook his head and I moved on, asking person after person until someone finally pointed at one of the smaller vessels moored by the dock. I hurried towards it, trying desperately not to break out in a run. As we drew closer, I noticed the crew members were moving around the deck, checking the ropes and disappearing from sight to load crates of cargo in the hold.

Within moments I stood before the gang plank, gasping slightly from the headlong rush, and adjusted my headscarf with trembling hands. Erik gripped Dolce's bridle with one hand and mine with the other, and I could tell that he was as nervous as I was.

'Out of the way!' A man roughly pushed me aside and I staggered sideways into one of the many crates. Erik cowered against Dolce as I yelped in pain. The man didn't pause and continued onto the ship, the roll of carpet across his shoulders hitting me squarely in the face.

'I'm looking for Captain Markus,' I said cautiously, one hand raised to my cheek to ease the stinging blow. The man grunted and moved away, but another figure moved forwards from the shadowed doorway where he'd been standing, arms folded and silently watching the proceedings.

'You've found him,' he said calmly, dark eyes giving me a brief glance up and down. 'If not from the process of elimination,' he continued, 'seeing as you've blundered your way up and down the docks asking anyone and everyone.'

I felt annoyance rise up and my chin raised defiantly, a retort forming on my lips. But then I bit my tongue, remembering that this man was the only hope we had to escape Scardia and time was running out. So, with great difficulty, I forced a smile and ducked my head a little.

'I pray you'll forgive my ignorance, but I am a stranger here. I need passage for myself and my brother across the Meridian. We also will need to take my – our – horse with us,' I corrected myself hastily before pushing on, 'we can pay you well for the crossing.'

I let my eyes meet his again and felt a shiver pass through me. His dark hair was tied back and his cheeks were rough with stubble, the faded shirt he wore was loose and flapped in the breeze. He was staring at me too intently, calculatingly, and I felt sweat begin to bead on my forehead. Erik was still behind me, thankfully silent, his hand gripped mine like a death-trap.

'I've already agreed to take one unwanted passenger on my vessel,' the Captain said slowly, 'already he's been causing issues with the crew. Give me a reason why I should agree to take more.'

I took a breath and let it out slowly, the wheels in my mind turning at full speed. How much should I tell him? What adequate story would he believe?

'We're going to stay with the only family we have left,' Erik said quietly as he moved out from behind my skirts and stood beside me. 'Our parents have recently died and now we have to move away.' His voice wobbled slightly, which may have been from fear but was hopefully interpreted as sorrow. I tried to look mournful and nodded in agreement. But the Captain was watching me even closer now, and my heart beat even faster.

'And there's the men who are following my sister,' Erik said matter-of-factly, and I froze in surprise before turning to stare at him in disbelief. How did he know about the Trackers? But my sudden terror was short-lived as he added, 'our parents had some debts, and the mercenaries who they borrowed money from wanted us as payment. When my parents refused, they were burnt in our home.' Gods, what kind of imagination did this child have? The horror on my face was mingling with incredulity now and I fought to master my emotions. Luckily for me, Captain Markus was staring at Erik now, apparently absorbed in the story. 'We barely had time to give them a proper burial,' Erik sniffed dramatically, wiping his nose on his sleeve, 'the mercenaries knew that we weren't there that day and they came after us the day of the funeral. We've been riding for hours just to get ahead of them.'

'So,' Captain Markus said, 'let me get this right. You believe that there are men coming after you, and so you wish to cross the Meridian? Most would say you were mad for wanting to do so directly after winter.'

'Mad I may be,' I said quickly, 'but we can pay you well.'

'How well?' He frowned.

'Twenty silver pieces,' I said confidently.

'Fifty.'

'Thirty.'

'Fifty.'

'Thirty-five and that's my final offer,' I said, my heart now beating with a strange exhilaration. The Captain gazed into my eyes for a moment, and then reached out a hand and I shook it in silent acceptance.

'You should bring the horse below now,' he said gruffly, 'and don't go expecting extravagant hospitality. We're a small vessel and we don't put on any airs or graces for anyone.'

'Thank you, Captain Markus,' I said quickly, 'for everything.' He probably would never know how much he'd saved us this day; how close the Trackers were to catching me.

He grunted something incomprehensible then said, 'don't call me Captain. Markus suits me just fine.' With that he stomped off, shouting out orders to several men around us, as we slowly led Dolce onto the deck and down to the hold below.

Chapter Eleven

I didn't know who the other unwanted passenger was for the first day of travel. Our cabin was adjoining his but all we knew was that his candles burned late into the night and he requested meals in his chamber. However, since Markus obviously didn't care for formalities, he did not oblige and so our neighbour went hungry.

I was glad to spend most of my time below deck, soothing Dolce with my voice and rubbing her down with all the tenderness and love I could manage. Erik quickly made himself useful, running messages up and down the ship and attempting to help in any way he could. When I wasn't comforting Dolce, I helped Viktor, the ship's cook, in the galley. Together we fed the others, who had voracious appetites which I wished I could reciprocate, however the continuous rocking motion of the boat sometimes made me queasy, especially at mealtimes. I avoided talking with the rest of the crew and went on deck infrequently, for that was Markus's domain, and after our first meeting I was eager to keep our interactions to a minimum.

After the evening meal I led Erik back to our cabin, which was a tiny space with two hammocks and a small chest in a corner. Thankfully we had a porthole which looked out at the grey waves. By the light of a lantern, I bent over a small book of Scardian lore and began to read. Erik watched me for a moment and then drew closer, peering over my shoulder.

Lisette chirped and ruffled her feathers, her tiny clawed feet digging into my skin through the thin fabric of my gown.

'What's it about?' He asked.

'It's full of different tales,' I replied absentmindedly, 'from stories of giants and the Drach-Mah to princes saving damsels from ogres' caves. There are valiant heroes and heroines who helped protect or save Scardia in some way or another, either from invasion or fantastical beasts.'

'It sounds fun,' Erik said, edging even closer.

'Do you want to read it?' I asked him with a smile as I held the book out. 'I've read it a million times.'

He shuffled his feet and glanced down, embarrassed, wrapping his arms around himself. I put the book down on my lap and watched him for a moment, wondering what I could do or say to ease the sudden awkwardness of the moment.

'You know,' I said quietly, 'if you want to be a knight you'll need to know how to read and write as well as hunting, riding and how to wield a sword.'

Erik stared at me mutely, and I continued, 'it's never too late to learn these things you know. I could teach you if you wanted.' It was my turn to look away now, as it suddenly occurred to me how much I wanted to be able to give this boy a chance at the future he wanted. How much it would mean to me to help him on his path and hopefully see him succeed.

'You'd do that?' Erik asked tremulously, and when I nodded, he gave me a brief hug. This was so surprising and sudden that I was caught off guard and Lisette flew off my shoulder, chirping shrilly. Erik pulled away and picked up the book, turning the pages reverently, gazing at the minute images alongside the paragraphs of text. I rose to my feet and strode to the door.

'Where are you going?'

'If you're going to learn how to read and write you'll need something to practice writing on,' I replied over my shoulder before exiting the cabin. Lisette stayed with Erik and I felt a little bereft to not have her comforting presence on my shoulder. I had some idea of where the captain's cabin was, but felt awkward asking for his help all the same.

Before I knew it, the wooden door was in front of me and I knocked nervously. Silence was the only answer for a few moments, and I had just turned to leave when the door opened.

'Are you lost?' His tone was curt and abrupt. Instantly I regretted coming here and stepped back.

'I was wondering if … if perhaps you had writing materials that I could borrow.' My voice quivered slightly, and I blushed as he stared at my face.

'Of course I do,' he said, 'but why would you require them?'

'I'm teaching Erik his letters,' I said.

'Then why didn't you have the required materials when you came on this vessel?'

'I … we … there wasn't time to buy more,' I stammered. Just the thought of going back into the seaside town after boarding the ship made me shiver even now, imagining the possibility that Trackers had already arrived and would be lying in wait, probably questioning the local inns and taverns to figure out where I'd gone.

Markus was watching me and I blushed once more, realising that my face was showing too much emotion and that he'd noticed.

'You'd better come in then,' he said, pushing the door wider. I stepped past and saw him stiffen; he didn't like me, of that I was sure. From his expression and posture, one might think that he considered me a threat to himself and all he held dear. I stepped away and pretended to ignore how he instantly relaxed. Annoyance rushed through me; it wasn't like I was a contagious disease or unbearable to be around. I didn't see why he had to act thus, after all, he'd accepted my money for passage, albeit grudgingly.

A lantern was burning on a low table, which was covered with maps and piles of books. An expansive bed spanned one side of the cabin, and I saw that it too had piles of books strewn over the covers. There were several windows which looked out on the dark waters below, which moved with a steady, constant beat. A screen was bolted down in one corner of the room, and I realised there must be a bathtub behind it. Envy joined the annoyance now, and I began imagining what it would be like to relax in a hot bath, a luxury I had long missed. A cough brought me to my senses; Markus was watching my quiet perusal of his cabin, arms folded and scowling.

'I was wondering if you had paper or a slate,' I said hastily, realising that he was waiting impatiently for me to leave. He moved over to the desk and opened a drawer, withdrawing a small slate and some pieces of chalk. As I took them from his outstretched hand, words of gratitude rising to my lips he said,

'You understand that this will add to the cost of your passage.' I nodded and pulled the slate, but he held it firm. 'And I'm beginning to reconsider the price we agreed on for your passage,' he said quietly, 'it's been a long time since I transported a horse in my cargo hold and I don't often have young children underfoot. Not to mention, the unluckiness of having a woman aboard a ship.'

I froze and snarled with fury. He'd touched a nerve, and he didn't realise how deeply this particular pain ran.

'We agreed on thirty-five silver pieces,' I snapped, eyes flashing, 'I'm willing to pay for the renting of the slate and the chalk, but nothing more.' I yanked the slate and chalk out of his hands vehemently. Turning on my heel I spun around and strode away, red hair flicking out from under my scarf with the abruptness of my exit. His laughter followed me and I gnashed my teeth furiously, cursing him in every expletive in each different tongue I knew. As I entered our cabin, Erik took one look at my face and cowered away, attempting to hide himself in his hammock. I forced a smile and placed the slate and chalk in the chest.

'That captain somehow seems to enjoy getting on my nerves,' I said with passable calmness, and Erik gazed at me warily for a second before asking,

'What did he say?'

'He wanted to extort more money for our passage,' I grumbled, rolling into my own hammock and sliding out almost as quickly onto the hard floor. Muttering one of my preferred expletives under my breath, I attempted it again and this time succeeded in remaining in the hammock, despite my aching behind.

'The man next door was making strange noises,' Erik whispered, eyes darting to the wall which separated our cabins, as though our neighbour would have his ear pressed against it to overhear our words. 'It sounded like chanting or something, and there was this banging.'

I raised my eyebrows in surprise, before I heard for myself that Erik was right.

The sound of stamping feet began, and it was accompanied by a low, muffled chant. The pitch turned to a shriek, ringing through the wall between us. A rumbling noise joined the overall cacophony which rose and fell, like the waves outside. I glanced at Erik, who was leaning back in his hammock.

'It was like this before?'

'Yeah,' he said, closing his eyes and, to my immense surprise, falling asleep. I waited a few moments before getting carefully out of my hammock, watching him warily, worried that he'd awaken as quickly as he'd fallen asleep. Luckily he didn't stir, and so I was able to change out of my clothes into a pale nightgown which was lying at the bottom of my pack. After days of sleeping in my clothes, it was heavenly to relax in something different, which didn't reek of sweat, dirt or horses. After another hasty glance which confirmed Erik's continuing slumber, I untied my headscarf. My hair had started to come loose from its plait, and, withdrawing a comb from my pack, I began to untangle some of the knots. As I worked, our neighbour began to reach notes I'm sure no man should ever attempt to reach. I could almost see the dividing wall beginning to vibrate with the repetitive beats of whatever it was he was doing.

My mind wandered, recalling what Markus had said to make me so angry. His comment about women bringing bad luck, although I knew it was a common misconception, had hurt more than he knew. I took a deep breath as I yanked hard on the comb and bit back a whimper as pain coursed through me. Markus didn't know that bad luck had followed me ever since that fateful day sitting by one of the palace fountains; he didn't know how dangerous it was to wish for things and then have them answered; he didn't know the guilt which followed and the pain of seeing those who sought to protect you cut down without a thought. Their faces flew through my mind: my parents, Lyn falling with an arrow in her back, Dora and Balgruf- a kind couple who had tried to shelter me shortly after that night, only to be killed before their time- and Keely. Thinking about Keely made a lump rise in my throat, and I wondered if I would ever see him again. As if sensing the turn of my thoughts, Lisette fluttered down next to me and gave a low chirrup.

My hands tied my hair, now knot-free, back into another plait and wound it around into a bun. I cursed myself for forgetting to buy something which would dye my hair red, or even some berries whose juice might conceal my identifying feature. I wrapped the headscarf back in place, covering the tell-tale white streak. There was another loud thump from next door and Lisette rose up, beating her wings wildly in fright. I clenched my jaw, the anger from before rising up again. Didn't he realise that we were trying to sleep? I'd had enough, either he quietened down for the night or I was going to demand that he moved cabins. There was a slight lurch in my stomach as I rose to my feet and staggered to regain my balance as the ship rocked momentarily.

My neighbour's door was barely a few feet down the thin hallway, and I rapped angrily. Almost immediately the strange combination of chanting, cawing, and foot-stamping came to an abrupt halt. I knocked again, louder this time and I heard feet coming closer. The sound of a lock clicked, and the door opened.

A skinny man with a monocle was standing before me, and I tried not to snort in laughter as I took in what he was wearing. His cloak seemed to be made of feathers, which matched the headdress of eagle feathers and shells roughly woven together. His light hair was crumpled beneath the headdress, and in one hand he clutched a strange block of wood which gave off the sound of rushing water when it moved.

'What,' I said without preamble, 'are you doing? Aren't you aware that the rest of us require sleep and rest?' As I spoke, I took in the state of his room, which was even untidier than Markus'. Pieces of parchment were scattered everywhere, and candles flickered from precarious positions on the table and floor. On the wall a strange picture of what looked like a compass had been painted in chalk, with bizarre symbols and runes surrounding it.

'I wasn't aware that I was causing any trouble,' the man said, offended. 'Besides, my studies are far too important to be interrupted, and you've already caused a great disturbance in the cosmos by barging in here.'

It took me a moment to register what he'd said before saying, 'I didn't barge in here. And I wouldn't have interrupted your studies if you were a bit quieter.'

'But the trans-morphic chant cannot be repressed,' the man said, 'you've cut me off from connecting with the spirits of nature and therefore their metamorphosis will be impacted.' His monocle fell down as he stamped his foot in frustration.

'What?' I asked bluntly.

'The spirits of nature require the trans-morphic chant to transcend between their multiple forms. Understanding these spirits and their reasoning is one of my many fields of study.' He pushed the monocle up, and resumed his monologue, 'they need to be communicated with no less than four times a day or else their anger will be boundless.'

'Surely all of this,' I gestured at the multiple books, scrolls and sheets of parchment, 'is not for these spirits.'

'My work spans multiple fields,' the man said brusquely, irritated at my apparent disinterest. 'But your presence is disrupting the required calmness of the soul which will appease the spirits. You come in here with accusations and blatant disregard for my work and I demand that you leave!'

I was stunned for a moment at how quickly his tone changed, and how his eyes bulged, a vein in his temple pulsing.

'I came in here to ask you to be quiet and respect the rest of us who have a right to sleep in peace,' I snapped, my temper rising once more. 'Surely that's not too much to ask.'

'Apparently it is,' a wry voice came from the doorway, 'I suggest you accept defeat and let Dylan continue with his … ritual.' I glanced up and saw Markus standing there, a definite smirk lurking on his darkened features.

'Yes, your intrusion here is pointless,' Dylan stated pompously, 'thanks to your interference I'm going to have to continue even longer to appease the spirits.'

I growled and stepped towards him, hands tightening into fists, and he stepped back, stumbling over his trailing feather cloak. Almost immediately Markus' hand was grasping my arm and leading me towards the doorway.

'By the way Dylan,' he said over his shoulder, 'I recommend that you have your meals with the rest of us from now on if you want to reach the Eastern Lands in good health.' Dylan gave a loud humph and closed the door behind us with a slam.

As soon as the door closed, I whirled around, half determined to go back and knock some sense into the man, but Markus' hand was still restraining me. Instead, I turned my fury on him.

'What gave you the right to come in and interfere? Let me go!'

'If two of my passengers are bickering it falls to me to sort it out, same as if there's a problem amongst the crew, and I won't let you go until you control yourself. The last thing I need is you causing more of a scene.' I glared at him and pulled away, but he held me firm.

'You're hurting me,' I hissed, pulling harder, and his fingers immediately loosened. It was such a surprise that I staggered backwards and nearly fell. Yet again he caught me, this time not to restrain me but to steady me. It took me a moment to realise how close he'd come and I stilled, unsure about what to do. For a second we stood there, inches apart, and I could feel the tension rising as I looked into his dark eyes. But then I realised that I was standing in my nightgown, and his hands were still holding me within inches of his chest.

'Thank you,' I mumbled, glancing away, and the moment was broken as his hands dropped. I turned and fled, closing the door behind me and leaning against it. Erik was still asleep, but Lisette's beady eyes watched me as I stood there, my breathing uneven as if I'd been running a marathon.

I blew out the lantern and stood for a moment in the moonlight which peeped in through the porthole. My feet moved over to my hammock and I rolled into it, wrapping the fabric around me, hoping that I wouldn't fall out again. I lay there for a while, staring up at the ceiling, listening to Dylan's strange chanting carrying on and on into the night. In my mind's eye I saw Markus in front of me again, in that moment when time seemed to halt and all that seemed real was the bare inches of empty air between us. A tightness rose in my chest and something I'd never felt before twinged in my belly. I let out a low huff of confusion and rolled over, letting the rise and fall of the ship lull me into a not deep, but at least long, sleep.

Chapter Twelve

Over the next few days I tried to avoid the captain, and it seemed that he too avoided me. However, I couldn't stop Erik from seeking him out, and was even pleased to see him agree to practice some basic thrusting and parrying with wooden swords on the deck. Gradually, Erik was coming out of his shell; his eyes brightened and his appetite increased until he ate almost as much as the sailors. The sound of his laughter warmed my heart, especially after remembering my brief encounter with the timid, cowering boy in Nuuk no less than a week ago. But after several days, I realised that I would need to raise the issue of bathing with him. It was becoming unbearable sharing a cabin with a boy who refused to wash himself, and every time I tried to raise the subject, he'd rush off to find one of the sailors to learn something new. It was with a heavy heart then, that I sought Markus out again. If the boy wouldn't listen to his big 'sister' then surely he'd pay attention to the captain.

'Never,' Markus declared when I'd explained the situation. 'Not in a thousand years.' His shock was so apparent that his face was devoid of its common wryness. He was leaning over one of the maps on his table, one hand clasping a compass which glinted in the sunlight.

'I can pay you,' I said desperately, 'he won't listen to me.'

'He's old enough to clean himself,' Markus objected, 'and besides you're his sister. If anyone should force him to be clean, it's you.'

'No,' I said before I could stop myself. He stared at me for a long time, and once more I got the impression that he was learning a lot more than I wanted him to. 'I mean,' I amended quickly, 'our mother always took charge of that and without her around, Erik is less likely to … well …' my voice trailed away into nothingness and I glanced around helplessly.

'Fine,' Markus said resignedly, 'but it'll cost you.'

A wave of relief washed through me and I smiled despite myself. We could haggle over the price later; all that mattered was that Erik would be clean for the first time in possibly months.

'Thank you,' I said, and turned away, not really noticing his stunned expression or his grunted reply.

That night Erik was casting me grumpy looks across his stew, but I pretended not to notice. I'd also pretended not to hear his desperate attempts to extricate himself from Markus' cabin as he encountered the bar of soap and Markus' bathtub. Yet he sat before me now, hair shining and his skin finally clean of all the dirt and grime which he'd worn like a second skin until now. Markus was also bearing marks of the fight, although grinning in an absent-minded way as though he hadn't really minded going to the trouble of cleaning Erik after all. As Erik gave a low humph and clanged his spoon against the bottom of his bowl, I couldn't resist smiling to myself. He really would have to learn how to adapt to bathing regularly if he was to continue being my 'brother'.

A sniff from the seat beside me made my lips tighten as I lifted my water glass. Dylan had left behind his parchment-strewn cabin and deigned to sit at the same table as us, more specifically, beside me. When he wasn't declaring the inadequacy of the meal, a point which both Viktor and I took offense to, he rambled on about his studies. After only ten minutes of his monologue, the majority of the crew had left in disgusted silence, no doubt to discuss amongst themselves the multiple reasons against taking passengers on these trips.

Markus stayed behind, neither adding to Dylan's incessant words nor starting a new conversation. I watched him out of the corner of my eye, aware of the moment when he rose to his feet and moved over to the stove.

'...But of course the Lord of Winterdale was so impressed with my works that he extended the invitation of being scholar-in-residence for the winter period as well,' Dylan was saying, 'it's thanks to his patronage that I was able to pursue my studies of the Gods of nature. And the Opium Sigilus, the pride of my collection, will help me to understand them. It took many long years to find it. I had to send out countless research assistants to retrieve it, but thankfully the Lord of Winterdale found me just the *right* man to do the job. And he desired an adequate sum for his trouble, along with a signed copy of my book on the importance of understanding the cosmos.' He seemed completely oblivious to our disinterest and the departure of the crew in general. Instead, he gazed into space, his monocle and its chain gleaming in the lantern light.

Markus had opened the door of the stove and was poking the charred pieces of wood inside. He slowly picked up some logs nearby and placed them in the stove, and when he spoke- his voice cutting through Dylan's monologue- his eyes never left the new flames which began to catch.

'Tell me, 'he said, 'is your Opium Sigilus different from any other parchment?'

'Of course,' Dylan spluttered, clearly offended at being interrupted, 'it depicts the exact location of the temple which Karl Hoarfist went to on his pilgrimage in—'

'Does it burn like any other parchment?' Our captain pressed. I felt my lips twitch in a smile. Erik burst out laughing as he looked from Markus' inscrutable expression to Dylan's purpling one.

'Well I never!' Dylan exclaimed angrily, 'the audacity … you have no idea how valuable this parchment is, it's worth more than your whole ship and belongings put together.'

'And yet you paid the adventurer who found it with a signed book,' Markus said calmly.

'He was a great admirer of my work!' Dylan snapped, and without another word, he stormed out of the galley. Now it was just the three of us remaining there, and I began to gather up the empty bowls. Over the past few nights, Viktor and I had decided that he would clean up the lunch and breakfast dishes, whilst I took care of the dinner ones. After working at inns, this job wasn't new to me, although it was a relief not to have to pour tankards of beer for men who'd attempt to get other pleasures than the alcohol they'd paid for. The dishes clanged in the sink and I filled a kettle with water and placed it on the stove to warm. Markus leaned back and watched, not offering to help or provide suggestions, which didn't bother me. I preferred being left alone after all.

I handed Erik one of the last, rosy-coloured apples and began to wipe down the large table with a damp cloth. It may not be up to my mother's standard of spotless cleanliness, but I didn't care. It was hardly likely that the sailors would mind either. When the water was heated through, I poured it into the sink and rolled up my sleeves, using the rag and soap to scrub each bowl. The steam was rising steadily, and I wiped away my hair, which was plastered across my brow. The movement nudged my headscarf aside and I absentmindedly pulled it back into place.

'If you're hot you can take that off you know,' Markus said, pointing at the scarf.

'I'm fine,' I said quickly, 'it keeps my hair out of my way and it's comfortable.'

'Is that why you sleep with it on?' Erik piped up from behind me and I paused for a moment, hand hovering over another bowl.

'You should know Erik,' I said with false calmness, 'that on this ship I don't like having my hair constantly down where it can get knotted so easily. I always wear my hair in a scarf, it's practical. Now if you've finished that apple, I want you to go and practice your letters in our cabin. I'll be along shortly.'

Erik shrugged and bounced out, still chewing on the apple core as he went.

'He didn't have to go so soon,' Markus said, and I could sense his disapproval.

'He's got a lot of work to do,' I said brusquely, 'after our parents died his lessons were sadly neglected for a while. If he wants to do well, he needs to know how to read and write.'

'So it's true that you even sleep in that thing?' I jumped at his change of tone, the sharpness which entered it as he glared balefully at my headscarf.

'Not always,' I replied stiffly, 'not that it's any of your business.'

'No,' he said, 'but that doesn't stop me from being curious. It's not every day that you have a pair of orphans on your ship crossing the Meridian.'

'No, I suppose it isn't,' I said.

'One thing I would like to know is how you found out that I was setting sail,' he continued, 'I wasn't aware that it was well known where I was headed. Unless, perchance, you ran into that scholar beforehand and he told you about our destination.' His mouth twisted and I smiled despite myself.

'No, I was told by a friend to ask for passage at the Seven Wastrels Inn, and the innkeeper told me to find you.' My voice wavered for a moment, as the last image of Keely's face crossed my mind, and shame filled my heart. Lisette chirped and fluttered onto my shoulder almost as if she sensed my change of thought.

'That's a strange bird,' Markus said quietly, 'the way it follows you around, almost like a protector.'

'Lisette's one of a kind,' I admitted grudgingly. As if sensing the change in conversation, Lisette began preening herself ostentatiously under his gaze.

'Where did you get her?'

'She belonged to a friend, and when he wasn't able to look after her anymore, he gave her to me.' My throat was tight and I wished he'd just go away. 'But my parents let me keep her.'

'You must miss them.'

If only he knew how much. I blinked, trying to chase away images of my mother, her strawberry blond hair tied back and pinned with rubies, her voice calm and assured whilst my father would swing me up in the saddle and ride with me through the palace gardens, laughing as I shrieked in delight.

'Yes,' I said, 'very much.' I washed the last bowl and dried it, stacking it away with shaking hands. It was a shock then when Markus' hands reached out and clasped my own. I stared, eyes wide, confused.

'I'm sorry about your parents, Karliah,' he said gravely, dark eyes gazing into my green ones. 'I hope the men responsible were punished.'

I laughed hollowly, 'if only that were possible.'

'What makes you say that?'

I didn't reply, hoping that the moment would pass over and that he would forget. Instead, I racked my brains for something that would distract him.

'What about your family? Were you always a sailor?'

His hands left mine as he leaned against the table, arms folding in his usual pose. I allowed myself to relax and my breathing slowly restarted.

'Dead.' His voice was hard. 'My father died in a storm at sea when I was eighteen. Our ship capsized over the Kraken's Mouth and his body was never found. I survived by clinging to some of the wreckage and a passing ship picked me up a day later. My mother didn't last long after he died, and then there was just me.'

'So you've been crossing the Meridian since you were eighteen?' I asked. The side of his mouth twitched upward.

'Long before that,' he said, 'I've been on ships ever since I could walk. And the Meridian is not always dangerous to cross.'

'Is it true that there are sea monsters in the Kraken's Mouth?' I asked, hoping that he wouldn't dismiss me with a laugh. Just thinking about the deepest ocean trench, which marked the borderline between Scardia and the Eastern Lands, made me shiver. Many people claimed that it was the deepest heart of the Meridian which separated the uncanny from the sane, a place which, once crossed, cast you into a world of magic and terror.

'Perhaps,' Markus shrugged, 'considering what they say about it, anything could be possible. But we haven't often seen creatures from the deep.'

I smiled, relieved, and began to move towards the doorway. It was time to focus on teaching Erik, and I'd ask him to keep his observations about my routine to himself. I didn't want anything more being said which would make Markus suspicious about our story. For a moment I paused on the threshold, wondering whether to say goodnight, and then moved on. There was a slight movement behind me but I didn't turn back. It was rare that we could have a conversation, and I didn't want to tempt fate by remaining any longer.

Chapter Thirteen

It was the rocking which awoke me. Outside was darkness, but I could hear the crashing of the waves and the howl of the wind. There was a loud crack and a jagged streak of lightning flashed across the sky, illuminating for a second our cabin. I rolled out of my hammock as the ship pitched to one side, and hit the ground with a resounding thump. There was a whimper from the corner of the room, and within moments Erik was clinging to me. I held him close, stroking his hair and murmuring words of comfort, wondering about the others. Over the sound of the wind and waves it was impossible to hear if anyone was on deck. I had to go and check, to see if everyone was alright.

'Stay here,' I said, and Erik nodded as I let him go. Lisette squawked in protest as I struggled to the door and out into the hall. The next step was to check on Dylan's cabin. I may not be particularly fond of the man, but it was only decent to check on him. I pounded on his door.

'Dylan?' There was no answer. I pounded again and paused; my ear pressed against the wood. From within the cabin, I thought I heard a faint groan.

'Dylan?' I tried the handle but it was shut firm, and so I threw my weight against it, almost losing my balance as it swung open. The ship lurched and I toppled forwards, clasping the door frame for support. Dylan was crouched on the ground next to a flickering lamp. I glanced around the room, recognising multiple objects from his dinner-time monologues. His maps, parchment and other strange objects such as his rain stick, Mioman paddle shoes and feathered cape were scattered around him in complete disarray. His face was pale and sickly, with every lurch he groaned and clutched his stomach.

'Are you alright?' I asked, and he gave a feeble nod, before pulling a bucket towards him. I turned and left, shutting the door behind me. The steps to the deck were slick with water and I braced myself for the storm outside. As I emerged from the deck below, the wind tore at my dress and the rain plastered my hair to my face within seconds. I saw our captain by the wheel, holding a rope in one hand and shouting incoherent words into the wind as the rest of the crew hurried back and forth. There was another clap of thunder as we pitched forwards over a wave, and lightning streaked across the sky once more. Markus saw me then, stood frozen at the top of the steps, and yelled something that I couldn't quite distinguish over the wind. He tried to indicate that I should return to the hold but as both hands were occupied, he could only use his head. With his head jerking sporadically back and forth he looked a bit like a half-crazed chicken. 'What are you doing here?' Markus roared.

'I thought you might need some help,' I called back, as the ship rolled to one side again. Behind Markus two crew members, whose names I vaguely remembered as Finn and Jor, had turned around at Markus' words and began yelling other words at me which I couldn't distinguish. But their meaning was clear- the deck was no place for a woman, especially during a storm.

A wave slammed over the side of the boat and struck my side, and I toppled. I was drenched through the icy water, as the wind rose to a gale. I was trying to get to my feet when another wave buffeted me again and I was slipping across the deck caught in the rush of water. I let out a terrified shriek and then hands gripped my upper arm and hauled me to my feet. I glanced up and saw Viktor looking down at me with an inscrutable expression. With a firmer grip than I would have imagined, he led me back to the hatch and forced me down the steps before closing it above me. I shivered in the darkness and hugged myself, trying to rub some feeling back into my arms.

I was halfway to my cabin when I remembered Dolce. I hadn't expected this sort of crossing when I insisted she come with us, she would be terrified. I slipped along the hallway and down another one, grabbing one of the lit lanterns from the kitchen. There was a pain in my chest as I hastened down another stairwell and opened the door to the hold. Even from the other side of the door I could hear her terror. Inside was darkness, but by the light of my lantern I could see her frenzied eyes from where she shuffled anxiously in her stall.

'It's all right, Dolce,' I said gently, 'we're going to be alright.' I edged closer towards her, murmuring calm and comforting words as the ship rocked. I spoke of happier times, before the Usurper, when we were not in constant fear of being hunted, when we would ride through the palace gardens beside Lyn or my mother. When I was close enough, I reached out and stroked her neck, all the while maintaining my stream of words, conjuring images of warm summer days, green pastures and her favourite treat of an apple. As the night drew on, the rocking began to cease and Dolce quietened, the fear in her eyes slowly receding. I didn't pay much attention to the passing of time and didn't hear any more noises from above deck, for I was caught up in the description of brighter times.

When sunrise came, the pale grey light filtering through the porthole, I deemed it safe to return to my cabin. My throat was parched and I could barely keep my eyes open. With a whispered goodbye, I picked up the lantern and carefully made my way back to the cabin. Erik had fallen asleep and Lisette's beady eyes snapped towards me as I closed the door behind me. She gave a low chirrup and ruffled her feathers in annoyance at my delayed return. I ignored the irritated clicking of her beak, rolled into my hammock and closed my eyes.

It seemed that I slept for only a moment when there was a loud crash and someone was shaking me awake, none too kindly.

'What in the name of the gods were you thinking? Don't you know how stupid, how idiotic you were—' I fell to the ground with a cry, jolting as I hit the hard wooden boards. Instinctively my hands rose to my scarf, checking that it hadn't fallen out of place.

'She went to make sure you were alright,' Erik's voice was tremulous, his timid nature resurfacing as Markus turned his furious eyes on him.

'She nearly got herself killed is what she did,' he snarled, and he pulled on my arm, yanking me to my feet. Despite myself I cried out in pain and shock, my mind still groggy with tiredness.

'You should never go on deck when there's a storm,' Markus snapped in cold fury, shaking me with each word. 'You have no idea how to help in a situation like that and you put your life as well as the lives of my men in danger. Don't be so stupid and careless again.'

'I…' I began, my voice a mere croak, but his baleful glare silenced me. He released me as quickly as he'd grabbed me and was out of the door without another word. Erik came and helped me sit back down onto my hammock. I didn't realise until he touched my arm that I was shaking.

'He's right,' I said quietly, 'I was stupid last night. But I didn't know that they wouldn't need any extra help.' Erik was silent, his eyes still wide with fear, and I held him close. It seemed that his demons, like mine, remained ever-present. Whatever Mr Macmillan had done to him in that god-forsaken inn continued to haunt him, it was clear from the way his shoulders drooped, to the clammy sweat which had broken out over his forehead. My eyes were brimming with tears, and I bit my lip to hold them back. The last thing I wanted was for Erik to see me cry.

'I wish that I was braver.' Erik's voice was a mere whisper, and I thought for a moment that he might be holding back tears too. 'I wish that I could be big and strong and that I could—'

'It's wisest if you don't make wishes,' I interrupted firmly, as my grip tightened involuntarily. 'Wishes are dangerous; they can make your deepest desires come true in the strangest circumstances or they can tear your world apart. It's best to not tempt fate by speaking those desires aloud.'

'What makes you say that?' He sniffed.

'There are many stories about what happens when mortals dabble in magic or are victims of it,' I replied evasively. Guilty memories were starting to resurface and I was too tired to keep them at bay.

'Tell me one,' he said, 'please Karliah.'

'I don't think that would be a good idea now,' I murmured. My eyelids were drooping in spite of myself, the shock from

Markus' visit was wearing off and now my body was demanding respite. 'I was up all night, Erik, I need to sleep.'

'What were you doing all night?'

'I'll tell you later.' Even my voice was starting to sound as exhausted as I felt. 'Why don't you go and see if there's anything you can help with on deck, Erik. No doubt they won't object to you going up there now that the storm's passed.'

He rubbed his nose on his sleeve and left with a shaky attempt at a smile. I felt my lips curve upward and then allowed myself to relax back into the hammock and, eventually, sleep.

I slept poorly. I tossed and turned, all the while under Lisette's watchful gaze.

My dreams haunted me. Once again, I relived that night where I saw my mother murdered in cold blood, where Lyn's body keeled over behind me as I fled into the darkness. I was always running, always fleeing the man whose face was in shadow, but who laughed as he watched my mother's lifeless body fall to the ground. Wherever I hid he followed, and I could almost feel his fingers gripping my wrist in sick triumph. Another figure was beside him, a man whose turban glistened with onyx and rubies. Whilst my pursuer was in shadow, this man was lit by the glow of the sun, and even in sleep the look in his eyes chilled me to my core. His teeth flashed white as he smiled, and I felt myself caught in his gaze, unable to look away.

Is this not what you wanted, little princess? The man asked, and although he did not open his mouth, I could hear his rich, deep voice resonating in my mind. *You have only yourself to blame for their deaths, if not for you it could have all been avoided. Look around you, all of these people lost their lives for you, just so that your wish could come true.*

And instantly I was surrounded by everyone I had ever known, and they lay as I had last seen them, eyes vacantly staring upwards towards the distant starlight. I didn't want to see this, to see how the Usurper had finished them after hours of torture, their lifeless bodies stretched as far as the eye could see. The sense of suffocation rose up, choking the breath from my lungs; the smell of blood, death and decay filled my nostrils and I began to cough, struggling to breathe.

Don't forget, little princess, the turbaned man smiled, *this is what you wanted.*

'No!' My denial came out as a scream and I jumped awake, shaking and sweating with tears already half-way down my cheeks. Lisette rose into the air, beating her wings and squawking in protest at my sudden outburst.

The door opened and the last person I wanted to see entered. His monocle was in its usual place and his strange, feathered cloak was dragging behind him.

'Would it be possible,' Dylan snapped, 'for you to refrain from shrieking like that? I'm in the middle of a very delicate part of my translation and I require absolute silence—' He cut off mid-tirade when he saw the tears on my cheeks. It took him a moment to figure out what to say next, and I could almost see the wheels in his mind turning. He blinked several times and I wiped a hand across my cheeks.

'Are you … alright?' The words sounded slightly distasteful in his mouth, or maybe he was just not used to showing any kind of feeling beyond arrogant superiority to other people. I nodded, unwilling to speak because I knew my voice would break. 'You don't look alright,' he said slowly, and I could feel his gaze boring into the side of my face, 'it looks like you've been crying.'

I bit back a sarcastic response and instead resorted to glaring at him. 'What's that?' His gaze had sharpened on a certain point near my left temple. I felt a wave of fear go through me as I reached up and felt that my scarf had slipped backwards. Almost instantly there was a loud squawk and Lisette took off from my shoulder heading straight for Dylan, beating her wings around his face so that he shied away. She gave me just enough time to fix my scarf before she returned to her perch and began preening her feathers, obviously very pleased with herself. Dylan was cowering in the doorway now, his hands still up near his face in case Lisette decided to swoop on him again. I tried to keep my features calm as he regained his composure.

'You were saying?' My tone was cool, but my heart was pounding with the fear of detection. Had he glimpsed the strand of white hair which I normally kept so well hidden? Would he connect it with the royal family?

'Nothing,' he grumbled, 'I must have imagined it. And it would be much better for everyone aboard if you got rid of that little bird.' He shot Lisette a look full of dislike, and then stalked back to his own cabin, closing his door with a petulant slam.

'She's a budgerigar,' I called out after him, 'and I'm keeping her for as long as she wants to stay with me.' There was a resounding thud from within his cabin and I grinned to myself, it was fun to tease the man.

With Lisette's proud chirps in my ear, I strolled to the galley to see if Viktor needed any help. Sure enough, the big lumbering man was peeling a small mountain of potatoes at the table. At my arrival he glanced up and then looked away, and I felt a twinge of guilt for the previous night.

'Thank you for saving me last night,' I said quietly as I took a knife from a drawer and began peeling potatoes alongside him. 'I'm sorry if I caused any trouble, I didn't realise that I would be more of a hindrance than a help.' It was a lot easier to explain myself to this giant of a man than the captain, whose rough shaking I had not forgotten.

He grunted something incomprehensible and smiled at me for a brief instant, before returning to the potatoes. We sat in companionable silence, and I was glad that Viktor was a man of few words. Our silence allowed the fear that had frequently raised its head that day to dissipate and I lost myself in the methodical work. Unfortunately, the lunch period came around all too soon and hungry sailors were pushing and jostling each other around the table as they were served simmering stew. They gave me surreptitious looks which revealed all too plainly their disapproval at my actions. As usual, I kept my head down and didn't talk to them, glad for the first time that up until now I hadn't gotten on friendly terms with any of them. I didn't think I could handle any more obvious disappointment in my ignorance. When Markus entered, his face dark and ominous, the conversation around the table stopped. Even Erik, who had been raptly telling me how he had climbed all the way up to the crow's nest and been allowed to use the telescope to check that no pirates were approaching, fell silent at Markus' expression and began shovelling down his stew. I shot him a reproving look, which I felt a sister would do if her brother seemed to forget his table manners. He raised his eyebrows questioningly at me and I sighed, resigned.

I could feel the captain's stare penetrating the side of my face, and my cheeks warmed. The stew was steaming and I blew on it, hoping not to burn my tongue as I swallowed. Stringy pieces of beef and fragments of carrot and potato slid down my throat and I gave a satisfied sigh. The regular meals on this ship were far better than my fare had been for the past few days, they far exceeded small handfuls of crushed red berries or seeds.

Suddenly, there was movement around me, as the sailors all rose as one and left, with Erik trailing after them. It seemed that Markus' presence had well and truly frightened off the crew. Well, I wouldn't let him intimidate me that easily. I clenched my jaw, and then resolutely continued my lunch, as though I hadn't noticed that we were the only ones remaining at the long table.

'You look like you didn't get any sleep,' he said gruffly.

'Not much, no,' I replied coolly, 'but then I doubt you did either.'

'You'd be right,' he said wryly, and it took all my willpower not to turn and look at him. 'I'm sorry for shouting at you this morning.' The last words were clipped and short, almost as though he couldn't bear to let them pass his lips.

I finished my stew but remained where I was, the spoon held loosely in my hand.

'You had a right to reinforce that my presence is not desirable during a storm,' I said quietly, 'but you shouldn't have hurt me or woken me by yelling in my ear. And it wasn't necessary to do it in front of Erik.' I stood up and walked over to the sink to begin washing up. Viktor had begun heating some water over the stove for me, and I reached out for it, winding my hands in my apron to avoid getting burned. I poured it into the basin and began dumping the bowls into the piping hot water. While I waited for it to cool, I began to wipe down the table, but froze when I turned around, cloth in my hand, to find Markus behind me.

I jumped and clutched the bench behind me. He stepped closer and I breathed in the scent of fresh soap. He had shaved since I had seen him this morning, and I was stunned by the sudden impulse to reach out and feel the difference, to trace the planes of his face with my hands.

'I didn't mean to hurt you, Karliah,' Markus said, and my heart leapt into my throat. He stepped even closer and I felt trapped. A part of me wanted to flee, to escape this dark, brooding man who chastised me one minute and apologised the next, whilst another part wanted to stay and press my head against his shoulder and take shelter in his arms.

He was barely a foot away now, and I could see my reflection in his brown eyes. Slowly, tenderly, he reached down and removed the cloth from my hand and placed it next to me. Then his fingers curled around mine and lifted my hand upwards. My breath caught in my throat as he gave a little lopsided smile and pressed his lips against the inside of my wrist. A tingle ran down my spine and I shivered.

'I'm sorry,' he murmured against my palm, his gaze never leaving mine.

'It's …' my voice wavered and died, as I saw something else in his eyes which both frightened and excited me. I swallowed and blinked several times, trying to regain control of myself. 'It's alright,' I finished awkwardly. His lips pressed to my palm, and I held my breath, wondering what he would do next. With incredible tenderness, which I would not have expected from the man who had so roughly shaken me awake, his other hand framed my cheek and pulled me even closer.

My gaze never leaving his, I relaxed and allowed my cheek to rest against his rough, calloused hand.

There was a loud cough behind us and I jumped, hitting the side of my hip against the bench. Markus didn't move but his grip on my hand tightened momentarily.

'I don't suppose Captain,' Dylan's loud voice was piercing in the silence, 'that you know where I could find decent supplies in the Eastern Lands? Perhaps you have a map of Lowton in your cabin, since I gather you are a man of some intellectual capacity.' Over Markus' shoulder, Dylan was giving me a look which made my insides twist. Markus brushed his lips over my knuckles and left me, indicating with a hand for Dylan to follow.

'Well,' Dylan said disdainfully as he turned to leave, 'it's clear to see how you're paying for your passage.' With his nose in the air, he followed Markus towards his cabin. I watched him go and felt a cold emptiness overwhelm me. Part of me wanted to run after Dylan and to slap him across the face for jumping to conclusions and being such an arrogant ass. Another part wanted to remember the light pressure of Markus' lips against my skin and imagine what might have happened next. I closed my eyes briefly for a moment and felt once more his rough palm lining the side of my face, and how it had made me feel safe, if only for a moment.

Chapter Fourteen

There was a loud crash from the side of the ship and loud shouts from the deck. I clutched the sides of the narrow hallway and staggered to maintain my balance as the ship lurched. Lisette flew from my shoulder with a piercing cry and all I saw of her was a flash of green feathers as she disappeared into our cabin. I followed, confused. As far as I knew the sea had been relatively calm after the storm, and Erik had been raving about the fine skies and sunshine from his position in the crow's nest at lunch. An iron fist clawed at my heart for a moment, as I froze in the doorway to the cabin.

The cabin was empty, save for a quivering pile of feathers on my hammock.

There was a monstrous roar from outside, and I rushed to the porthole window. It didn't seem to be raining, but the surface of the ocean was bubbling and swirling. The water was dark and murky and then there was a loud splash which muffled the sound of more screams.

'Lisette,' I murmured through numb lips, 'I think there's something out there.'

The budgerigar answered with a faint chirp which seemed to summarise in one tremulous note how I was feeling. But it seemed that Lisette was not the only one to hear me, for, as if in response to my words, something leapt out of the churning dark water. It was a huge mass of scaly flesh and small wriggling legs. I screamed and fell backwards as the creature disappeared from sight.

Lisette was now sheltering underneath the hammock, and I didn't blame her.

'I thought Markus said that they weren't normally troubled by creatures of the deep in these waters,' I whispered to her. A cold fear was spreading through me, clogging up my throat and making it hard to breathe.

'Erik,' I glanced around the cabin once more, verifying that it was completely empty. 'He's out there, Lisette. He's not safe. What if that creature—' I cut myself off before I finished the awful thought. 'I have to get him.'

Time seemed to slow down as I pulled on my father's cloak, the one garment which would give me the courage to expressly go against Markus' wishes and into harm's way. I sped towards the deck, my thoughts fixated on Erik's face. I muttered a prayer under my breath, begging the gods to spare this boy, who, even though he was not my brother, had somehow wormed his way into my heart in these past few days. I couldn't bear to lose anyone else.

The deck was covered with water and broken pieces of railing. The crew were running everywhere, it took me less than a second to spot Markus, who was near the helm, a crossbow in his hands. He loaded a bolt and fired as the monstrous creature reared out of the water. Its scales glinted a sickly green and fourteen pairs of yellow eyes gazed down at us. The creature's face was framed by a frill and six smaller heads which pushed against each other and hissed. Tongues flicked between fangs the size of my forearm. It swooped down and caught one of the crew before throwing him high into the air. His scream mingled with mine as I stood paralysed, unable to think beyond my terror.

Erik. The thought pierced through my fear, and I was able to move again and look around the deck with purpose from my position near the stairs. There was no sign of a small cowering body anywhere, and I began to fear the worst. It would have been only too easy for such a small boy to be knocked overboard by the monstrous creature.

'Erik!' I shouted, 'Erik!'

A feeble cry answered my call and, with a heavy heart I raised my eyes towards the top of the mast.

'Oh no,' I murmured. There was another roar and the ship rocked as the creature smashed over the side, sliding across the deck with its hundreds of scaly feet fighting to slow its progress so that it didn't fall back in the water. The tail thrashed everywhere, hitting sailors over the side and knocking out even more of the deck's railing. I took my chance while the creature became occupied with Markus and some of the crew who had armed themselves.

I slipped a little as I hurried across to the rigging which led towards the crow's nest where Erik hid. The rope was slippery and rough in my hands as I forced my way upwards, clinging tightly with each step. There were shouts from below and I could imagine the look on Markus' face as he glanced up and saw me, skirts and cloak billowing in the wind as I blatantly disregarded his orders. I didn't have the strength to look back, my whole body was shaking with the strain of pulling myself upwards and I was sure that if I glanced back I would fall. Instead, I struggled onwards and glanced up to see Erik's white face staring at me as I drew gradually closer.

When I clambered over the edge of the crow's nest, I opened my arms and Erik clung to me, whimpering.

'It's alright,' I said in his ear, 'we've just got to climb down and go back to the cabin and we'll be safe.' It didn't surprise me that he shook his head into my side and wouldn't move. I pulled him with me to the side and peered down.

I soon wished that I hadn't. The distance between the crow's nest and the deck seemed even further from this angle. The cries and shouts from the crew pierced the air, and I saw that all their efforts to attack the creature were to no avail. Nothing seemed to be able to penetrate its scaly hide, in fact their attempts only provoked the creature more. One of its seven heads swiped at Markus and I screamed, one hand clutching the edge of the crow's nest while the other held Erik. Markus dodged to one side, cutting at it with a long blade. It veered away and turned, sliding across the deck and rising adjacent to the mast until it faced us. Erik's scream mingled with the wind, while I was struck dumb, staring into the multiple yellow eyes and seeing miniature versions of myself reflected back.

Erik's hand clutched mine as the creature let out another hissing roar. Its fangs dripped venom onto the mast and the deck below, as the seven heads waved back and forth almost as if it was trying to mesmerise us. The wind was rising now and I felt the knot of my headscarf slip away. My hair was released from its material prison and began to tear around in the wind, dancing in time with the flicking tongues. Erik was cowering beside me, and so he didn't notice the creature's heads freeze. The strand of white hair whipped across my face, melding with the red, but I was too afraid to pull it back and hide it.

The creature stared at me, roared again, and then catapulted backwards into the ocean with a loud crash. Slowly my breathing returned to normal, and I ducked down in the crow's nest, grabbing my headscarf from the ground and forcing it over my head before anyone could see. Erik had his eyes clamped tight shut and was muttering something to himself, still huddled at my side. I breathed easy when my hair was once more hidden, although I would have to tie my hair back again when I went back to the cabin.

'It's gone,' I said, my voice shaky with relief. 'We can go down now.'

Erik didn't say anything, but watched as in the distance the creature leapt out of the water and splashed away, its roars fading into silence. I led him to the side and began the descent with shaking arms. It took a lot longer than I thought, perhaps because my muscles had seized up with delayed shock, making it incredibly painful to move.

Erik reached the deck before I did and he waited at the bottom, as did Markus, who had barked out some orders to the rest of the crew who were trying to tidy some of the damage. When I was close enough, Markus reached up and lifted me down under Erik's nervous scrutiny. His face was even whiter than Erik's, and there was a long gash across his upper arm which had stained his shirt red. I was shaking from cold and shock and leaned against Markus' chest as soon as he had placed me firmly on the slippery deck.

'I couldn't find Erik,' were the first comprehensible words I choked out, 'I had to find him and get him back.'

'And that was why you disobeyed my orders?' His voice was low and gentle in my ear, and I was momentarily surprised that he wasn't shaking me or yelling in anger like he had earlier that day. I nodded and stumbled as I began to shiver violently. Markus looked concerned and caught me, not that I minded.

'When that monster rose up towards the crow's nest none of us could see what was going on. I thought for a moment that…' He trailed off and then said briskly, 'come with me, you need a hot bath.'

Erik trailed behind us, clearly fearing a reprimand for staying in the crow's nest. Yet for all the attention Markus gave him, it was as though he wasn't even there. It took me a moment to realise that Markus was leading me towards his own cabin.

'I'm fine,' I said awkwardly.

'You're frozen,' Markus replied jerkily, 'and you're in shock.'

I couldn't think of any retort quickly enough before we were standing in front of his door.

'Erik, you can wait for your sister in your cabin.' Markus' eyes remained fixed on me as we continued, and I gave Erik a weak smile as we left him behind. Markus opened his cabin door and ushered me inside.

'Wait here while I go and get some hot water,' he said, 'I won't be long.'

He was true to his word, although I think he might have just ordered a crew member to get the water in his stead, for he was back within several minutes of leaving. I had sunk down onto one of the chairs near the desk, eyeing the bathtub behind a screen. I wondered if Markus would leave when I took a bath, as propriety would dictate he should, or if he would stay.

His desk was scattered with maps and sheets of parchment, some of which were covered in a long, scrawling hand in black ink which was indecipherable. Piles of books were placed next to them, and I opened one absentmindedly which described the Scardian connections with other lands. I knew that to the south there were many other lands, which I had barely heard of, save for those hours either in my tutor's presence or in the palace library. They had strange names which sounded odd on my tongue when I tried to speak them: Karshka, Velkra and Felshkar. They were places of desert, swamps and ever-stretching forests. They differed greatly from Scardia, the land which had snow-peaked mountains all year round and glaciers which ran from the northern mountains to the sea. It was on one of those glaciers that my ancestor was crowned the first king of Scardia, uniting the land under the Ice Flame.

Absent-mindedly I touched the strand of hair that remained hidden under my scarf. Some had said that the strand of white connected us to the land, and so we could never leave Scardia forever. We were bound to protect it, our home, be it from invaders or natural phenomena. Others said that my ancestors struck a deal with the spirits and were cursed with an obligation to remain in the land of ice and snow. A wry smile tweaked my mouth as I imagined my ancestor, the High King Ulthor, a man of legend, and how he would react if he could see me now. What would he say if he knew that the final living heir to the Ice Flame was hiding from her true identity and fleeing to the Eastern Lands? Would he be ashamed that I had remained hidden for all these years, too afraid to take on the Usurper and regain my birth right? Would he be proud that I had escaped detection for so long? Or would he be angry that I was leaving my homeland for who knew how long?

The sound of Markus returning broke me out of my brief reverie, but something on my face must have remained for he asked, 'what's the matter?' He pulled the other chair closer to mine and held my hands loosely in his. When I didn't answer he said, 'it'll be alright, we'll be in Lowton in a couple of days.' He had cleaned the gash across his arm in the time away, and changed out of his shirt. There was a bulge beneath his sleeve and I gathered that it hid a bandage.

I glanced away, as Viktor and several other crewmen entered, carrying buckets of steaming water. Without a word they tipped them into the bath and left, shutting the door behind them. Markus rose to his feet and moved around the desk, taking his chair with him and gesturing at the screen.

'You can freshen up,' he said, 'I won't peek.'

I moved like a sleepwalker towards the bath and took refuge behind the screen. My clothes fell to the ground in a tangled heap and I cautiously stepped into the water. Heat overwhelmed me as I sank down into the bath, and I felt my muscles slowly begin to relax. I couldn't remember the last time I'd had a hot bath, for I had spent so long washing myself with a basin and cloth. The water was scented with something floral, and I stretched out languorously, relishing this small luxury. I untied my scarf and let my hair hang loose into the water, glad for the screen's protection. I trusted that Markus would keep his word and not watch me.

'What are you planning on doing in Lowton?' Markus asked suddenly, 'you said you had family there. Do they know that you're coming?'

I was too tired to think of making something up, and so tried to stick to the truth as much as possible. 'No, they don't know that we're coming. I barely know them; all I know is what my parents told me.'

'What quarter of town do they live in?' His tone was politely interested, but I was sure that he was a lot more interested than he was letting on.

'I can't remember,' I replied, hoping that he wouldn't ask anymore questions, and so I came up with some of my own.

'How long will you be docking in Lowton? Are you going to other ports in the Eastern Lands before returning to Scardia?'

'We have cargo to unload in Lowton,' he said, 'which will take a few days. Then we will continue along the coast to Knightbury. From there I'm not sure where we'll go, wherever the wind takes us I expect.'

'That sounds adventurous,' I murmured, before I ducked my head beneath the water again. When I re-emerged I heard his bark of laughter.

'Adventurous? Hardly. I go wherever I can get a decent commission and sometimes you find them in the most unlikely places. That's why I'm constantly on the move.'

'You never know what will be waiting just over the horizon,' I said quietly, a painful desire sinking its well-sharpened claws into my chest. 'You're lucky that you're free to follow your heart where it leads you,' I continued, 'you can keep exploring and doing what makes you happy until the end of your days.'

'As can you too, I'm sure,' Markus said. It was my turn to laugh, and it sounded harsh in the silence.

'I can't do any of that,' I said, my mouth twisted in a grimace, 'I never had the freedom you do. It's impossible to be an independent woman in these times, especially when you've got a young brother.'

'He's not that young,' Markus said, 'within a year or two he will be able to become an apprentice to some trader or craftsman.'

'Perhaps,' I said, 'if those pathways appeal to him. I don't want to hold Erik back from his dreams and I will do everything possible to help him achieve them.'

'But what about your dreams?' Markus' voice was low.

'I learnt a long time ago that dreams only bring pain and disappointment,' I tried to keep my voice steady, 'and my dreams, when I had them, were unable to come true.'

'What were they?'

'To have my parents back,' I whispered, 'to be safe and happy again. To meet someone who would accept and love me for who I am.'

'And who's to say that those last two wishes cannot come true?' His voice was as quiet as mine had been. 'Perhaps they could come true sooner than you believe.' His words made heat rush to my cheeks which had nothing to do with the steaming bath water. There was a movement from the other side of the screen and the door closed, signalling Markus' departure. I stared at my toes, peeping out of the water, deep in thought.

Of course, it was easy for Markus to say that my dreams were possible, and so they might be if I really was Karliah Merryweather, a peasant girl with a young brother. But it wasn't easy for Wilhelmina Fiordlasher, the lost princess to the Ice Flame. What would Markus say if he knew? Would he hate me for my deception? Turn me over to the Trackers and the Usurper? Or would he accept me, as in my latest daydreams I had imagined he would? I fingered the white strand in my hair, thanking the gods that the crew hadn't noticed it earlier. I couldn't afford to take risks, and I had been mindlessly ignoring my three rules.

'It would be best if you keep to yourself for the next few days until we reach Lowton,' I muttered to myself, 'that way you stop tempting fate and will stay out of trouble. Don't forget to keep your head down and keep your hair covered. No matter how you've been getting on with some people on this ship, it would be foolish to trust them with the truth, especially in these times. The Usurper's spies could be anywhere, just waiting for you to show yourself. Think about what happened to Keely – you can't run the risk of the same thing happening here.'

Erik was waiting in the cabin when I returned a good hour later, completely refreshed and relaxed, with my hair dried and once more under its scarf. As soon as I closed the door he said,

'Why did that monster just leave? One moment it was swiping people off the deck and the next it was gone. I thought we'd be its next meal when it began roaring at us.' I sat down on my hammock and Lisette fluttered onto my shoulder with a resounding chirp, which said quite plainly that I had been gone quite long enough and she would appreciate it if I didn't wander off without her.

'I don't know why it left,' I said, scattering some seeds onto my hand and offering them to Lisette, who accepted the gift and leapt down onto my palm. 'I really don't know.'

'It was so strange though,' Erik continued, 'it left so suddenly. Do you think it'll come back?' The last word was a tremble and I looked over at him.

'It's alright to be afraid,' I said quietly, but at my words he shot me an angry glare.

'I wasn't afraid,' he snapped, jumping to his feet, 'it didn't scare me.'

'Of course you weren't,' I smiled, trying to not sound too patronising, 'but it scared me. I think anyone brave, like knights or kings or wizards, have fears and succumb to them from time to time. It's not a sign of weakness, it reinforces their humanity.'

Erik was silent for a while, watching Lisette sort through the seeds before eating her favourites.

'You took a long time,' he said, and I was surprised at the surliness in his tone, 'what were you doing?'

'I was taking a bath,' I replied, wondering why he was so interested, and then hoping that Dylan hadn't been spreading rumours about what he'd seen. I certainly hoped he had kept his mouth shut. 'Markus and I were talking for a while and then I was able to wash and dry my hair. My hair always takes a long time to dry properly and since I was alone, I figured I would take advantage of the time. I didn't want to leave drops of water all over our cabin.' I shot him a cheeky smile which he reluctantly returned. 'I don't think he'll mind if you go and wash yourself. The water may not be as hot as it was, but it would do you some good to clean up after earlier. When you come back, we might go down and make sure Dolce's alright.'

Erik didn't say anything but left as quick as an arrow and I grinned.

'I don't understand other people sometimes,' I told Lisette, 'I really don't.'

She ruffled her feathers in acknowledgement of my words and fluttered back to my shoulder, clearly having eaten her fill. I returned the remaining seeds to the small pouch by my hammock and stroked her wings with the tip of my finger. My mind wandered to Markus and whether it would be wise to seek him out and thank him. I shook my head, dismissing the idea, I didn't want there to be any more cause for gossip. Besides, if we were to be arriving in Lowton in the next couple of days then we would be on our way and would have to say goodbye to Markus. My insides twisted at the thought.

'It would be better if I didn't try to imagine anything more than is realistic,' I said to the budgerigar, 'the idea of

something … anything between us would be impossible.'
Treacherously, I remembered the feeling of his arms around
me, lifting me down onto the deck and the stark relief on his
face to have me safe. I remembered the tender kisses he had
pressed against my palm, and I held it now, rubbing the skin
with my fingers, wondering how it would feel if he kissed me
again. How it would feel to feel his lips on mine and to wind
my hands through his hair and hold him close.

Lisette squawked, as if to remind me to stop imagining
things that couldn't happen. Unfortunately, the loud noise did
just that. She squawked several more times, to ensure that my
mind didn't wander off again.

'Can we go and rub Dolce down?' Erik had reappeared,
his hair damp and his eyes bright. Obviously, he hadn't taken
the time to relax in the water.

'Lead the way,' I said, and Lisette fluttered off with a chirp.
'I wasn't talking to you, Lisette,' I huffed as we followed the
green bird towards the hold.

Dolce was still agitated, and together Erik and I set about
calming her. It took a long time before she would let us rub
her down and tend to the grazes where she had scraped
against the stall in an attempt to escape.

'Will Markus come with us when we leave?' Erik asked as
he handed me some damp cloth.

'I doubt it.' I tried to keep my voice devoid of emotion,
'he has other jobs to do, and besides we paid him to take us
across the Meridian and no further.'

'But he likes you,' Erik mused, 'and I think he likes me too.
He's teaching me how to fight. I even disarmed him the last
time we practiced.'

I didn't have the heart to tell Erik that he had only disarmed Markus because he had been distracted, returning my smile while I was doing some work on deck.

'He let you use his bath,' Erik continued, 'and he doesn't let just anyone use it.'

'I was in shock,' I answered mechanically, 'he was just doing what any captain would do for his guests.'

'I don't think he'd let Dylan use his bath,' Erik said seriously, and I laughed.

'I'm sure that something about the bath would disagree with one or other of the spirits, and Dylan can't upset them.'

Erik laughed before returning to the topic which I had hoped he would forget. 'But Markus has been asking where we'll stay when we arrive in Lowton, and he said that we can stay on board until we have lodgings.'

'That was generous of him,' I said warily.

'And you haven't even told me what we're going to do once we get to Lowton,' Erik said eagerly, 'where will we go? Who are we really going to stay with?'

'We'll find lodgings at an inn until I figure out where to go next,' I replied, 'I need to find a way to contact my family. But I don't know where they live or how to reach them, so I'll have to ask some questions when we arrive.'

'It's a mystery,' Erik's face lit up, 'a quest. We have to discover their whereabouts.'

'Yes, I suppose so.' There was no way that I was going to reveal to Erik who my family was. Not until we had left the ship, and its highly appealing captain, behind us.

'Excuse me for interrupting your ... *riveting* conversation,' Dylan's disdainful tone identified him from the first syllable, 'but I have been sent to inform you that it is time for dinner. And apparently you shall be dining in the captain's cabin, while the rest of us,' he heaved an indignant sigh, 'shall be eating in the galley, as usual.'

'I told you Markus liked us,' Erik whispered as Dylan stalked away, 'he's just jealous that he can't have whatever we're having.'

'I should have been helping Viktor,' I said guiltily, as we followed Dylan's retreating back.

'He seemed to manage cooking for the crew before you came along,' Erik said bluntly as we reached Markus' door. I shrugged and then knocked.

The door opened and Markus smiled at us. I was so unused to his smile, that it took me a moment to realise that he was gesturing for us to sit down around his table, which had been cleared of the books and maps and was now set for three. It struck me as very odd that we were being invited to dine in the captain's cabin, especially since up until now everyone had eaten together, regardless of rank.

'Have a seat,' Markus said, holding out a chair for me. I shot him a confused look as I sank down, wondering what he was up to. When we were all seated, Markus poured wine into two goblets and half a goblet for Erik. He winked at the boy with no semblance of irritation for what had happened earlier, perhaps he had realised that it was no more Erik's fault for being on deck than anyone else's.

'Here's to surviving a horrific day,' Markus said, and we clinked goblets. I tried to ignore the way his eyes remained on me as we drank. Erik spluttered as he took a large gulp.

'Steady on, Erik,' Markus laughed, and thumped him on the back. The motion only made Erik cough more.

'Why do people drink that?' He asked when he finally had his breath back, 'it's disgusting.'

Markus pretended to look offended, 'this happens to have been a very good year for this grape.' I smiled, and took another sip, appreciating the smooth rich texture of the wine sliding over my tongue. It had been such a long time since I had tasted wine and I was almost tempted to close my eyes to savour it more. Erik had pushed his goblet away from him with a repulsed look. At that moment, a rather grumpy crewman entered, carrying a large tray weighted down with bread, butter and soup. I stared, wide-eyed, wondering when we had gotten bread and butter, since I hadn't seen it in the galley earlier. The soup was leek and potato, and smelt delicious as it was ladled into our bowls. Markus muttered something to the crewman as he left, and the man nodded, before closing the door.

None of us spoke for a while as we ate, relishing the hot soup and fresh bread and butter. Of course, Erik ate his soup as though his life depended on it and had soon cleaned his bowl, well before Markus or I had finished. He stretched back in his chair and glanced around the cabin with avid interest.

'Why did you want to be a captain?' He asked, as he began chewing another piece of bread. Markus glanced at him, surprised.

'I was raised by my father who expected me to follow in his footsteps,' he said, 'when he died, I naturally took over the business and continued to transport items back and forth from Scardia to other lands. We mainly travel to other ports in Scardia, but longer trips are sometimes necessary.'

'Like this one?' Erik said keenly. Markus nodded, and then served some more soup into our bowls. 'What are you taking to the Eastern Lands then?'

'Oh, a variety of objects,' Markus shrugged, 'silks, furs, wine, and let's not forget the Lord of Winterdale's favourite scholar and the important instruments for his research.' His voice was heavy with sarcasm and this time I couldn't hold back my laughter.

'Dylan wasn't very happy at coming to fetch us,' Erik grinned, 'I think he would have liked to have a private dinner away from the crew as well.'

'Well, he didn't go through the same harrowing experience that you did today,' Markus said, 'instead he complained that I didn't think of getting a sample from the creature for his studies.' He shook his head in astonishment, 'that man is unbelievable. He didn't even care that we lost five good men today. He just said that we provoked the monster into attacking us and made it worse for ourselves.' His mouth twisted and he looked away, scowling. The earlier light mood around the table had dissipated as quickly as it had come, and I noticed Erik shift in his seat uncomfortably. I reached over to Markus and laid my hand over his. Almost automatically, his hand shifted underneath mine so that he could clasp it.

'Your men were doing the only thing they could under the circumstances. That creature was savage; you had no choice but to defend yourselves.' His eyes met mine, and I saw in them the guilt and pain which he had been trying to hide. 'Did they have families?' I asked tentatively.

'Some did,' Markus said, 'Bryan and Mikael both had broods of children as well. But I'll provide for them, it's only right.' I squeezed his hand gently and he returned the pressure.

'Have your ships ever been attacked before?' Erik asked, and yet again the light of curiosity dawned in his eyes.

'Not quite like today,' Markus replied, clearly relieved at the subtle topic change. 'Mainly we just have issues with pirates. We've had a few skirmishes with them, but mainly they back down when they realise that we're willing to fight to defend our cargo.'

'Do they attack often?' Erik pressed, 'how many can you take on at once? Do you just wound them, or do you fight to kill? How much blood—'

'Erik!' I interrupted, shocked. 'That's enough.'

'What's it like,' Erik continued as if I hadn't spoken, 'to kill a man? Does it feel different to kill someone in the middle of a fight than when they aren't armed? What do you think when you see his blood gush from the wound—'

'Why are you suddenly so interested in blood and killing?' I snapped, unnerved, 'now is not the time to be asking such things. Bloodshed and murder are horrific things to experience let alone to be talked about with such … passion. If you don't settle down, you can go back to our cabin.' I folded my hands in front of me and frowned at the boy, he glowered back.

'You can't tell me what to do,' he said, 'or what to ask about.'

'You can ask, Erik,' Markus said smoothly before I could reply, 'but considering what happened today, and out of respect for those men who died, it would be wise to ask them at another time. It might also be better, perhaps, not to ask for gory details over dinner.'

'And it would be wise not to imply that your host knows what it's like to kill someone in cold blood,' I added quietly, trying to control the shock and anger that Erik's words had awoken within me. His intensity and fascination scared me, for I couldn't understand them. Thoughts of killing and murder brought back too many memories for me to want to spend time pondering on them. And then he riled my anger through his insinuation that Markus had harmed people in cold blood. What on earth was the lad thinking?

Deep down, a part of me recognised that my anger at Erik's words was because it was about Markus. The idea of someone insulting him, even to the smallest degree, made me want to defend him. I didn't want to hear things being said about him, especially when he had been so gentle and kind this afternoon. He may be abrupt, surly and have a temper to match my father's, but I wouldn't believe that he was a bad man. And to me, the idea that he could kill someone in cold blood was absurd.

But then, another part of my mind whispered, I often can't distinguish a murderer from a normal man; look after all at what had happened to my parents. They had been betrayed and killed by a man who had been on several of their main councils. Someone I once thought of as an uncle, even though he was not related to me. My hand trembled on the stem of my goblet as the image of my mother's inert body slumped against the wall flashed across my mind. She had been killed in cold blood and the man who did it had not even faltered as he drew the knife across her throat.

I blinked rapidly, trying to prevent the heavy tears which were clamouring to be spilt. I took a few deep breaths and barely spoke another word for the rest of the evening. Markus and Erik didn't appear to notice my silence, and instead amused themselves with stories of a time when pirates had grossly underestimated the ship's crew, and of the sea battle which followed. It was a way to answer some of Erik's questions without going into gory details, and for that I was grateful. The last thing I wanted right now was to hear about how other men had died, or of other grizzly images of pain and death which had occurred on the deck. My own memories played through my mind, making me unable to concentrate on Markus' tale. Before I knew it, the bowls had disappeared and Erik was yawning. I forced a smile as Markus caught my eye, but I got the feeling that he could see through my pretence.

'I think we should intrude no longer, Erik,' I said, 'after today we all need our rest.' We rose to our feet and Markus opened the door, still watching me keenly, a frown crinkling his forehead.

'Thank you for the evening,' I said as Erik began to lead the way out the door, 'it was very pleasant.' As I made to follow him, Markus touched my arm lightly.

'Are you alright?' His voice was low enough that Erik would not be able to hear. 'You were quiet for most of the night.'

So he had noticed.

'I'm fine,' I said, wishing that it could be true.

'You mustn't let what Erik said upset you,' he continued, 'young boys are often interested in violence. It's natural.'

I stiffened. 'Murder is not natural. No one should have to live in a world where it is considered such.' With that I stalked off, the painful memories which had arisen during the evening clamouring in my ears to be heard. There was a movement behind me as if Markus was going to follow, but he didn't, and I continued on. I closed my cabin door and moved over to my hammock.

Erik was already curling into his hammock. He whispered goodnight and turned away before I could reply, perhaps nervous in case I told him off again. Lisette fluttered onto my shoulder and chirped softly, as if to check that I was alright. Her beady eyes gave me an inquisitive look as I brushed her yellow and green feathers with the tip of my finger. I sighed and lay back, dislodging Lisette from her perch. She flew over to where the hammock was attached to the wall and settled herself on the iron ring, ruffling her feathers indignantly.

My anger had dissipated as abruptly as it had arrived, and now I was left just feeling empty. I was exhausted and wanted nothing more than to sleep, but thoughts kept flitting through my mind, denying that peaceful oblivion. The Usurper was laughing behind my eyelids, taunting my mother while I watched through a keyhole. My father was reaching down to lift me onto the saddle in front of him, his long cloak whipping in the wind behind us as we raced through the gardens, my laughter ringing in my ears. Lyn held me in her arms as I cried, her soothing words telling me that my parents would be back from their trip soon, and that when I was older I would be able to leave the palace grounds. My sobs escalated and I was sure that they weren't coming back, because of the way they kissed me goodbye and the look in their eyes as they left.

Keely chased me, screaming out for me to stop, to wait for him. As I turned, dark hands reached out, silencing him and dragging him out of sight. As I watched, terrified, the hands stretched out towards me, and grabbed at my hair as I ran. The headscarf I wore fell away and then the air was filled with crossbow bolts, cutting through my skin. There was a pain in my arms and chest and I was sure that I was hit. As I fell down, it was into the gaping mouth of a creature with long teeth and seven frilled heads.

I awoke with a start, lying against the hard wooden floor. The cabin was dark and silent, save for Erik's slow, deep breathing, and I lay on the ground, my arms aching beneath me. I rolled over to face the ceiling, gasping as my heart rate returned to normal. There was no way that I wanted to go back to sleep, not when my demons still reached for me whenever I closed my eyes.

Instead, I left the cabin, shutting the door quietly behind me. I had the vague idea of getting some water, but mainly I just wanted to move and forget my nightmare. My feet padded silently towards the galley, one hand guiding me along the wall. To my surprise someone was already there, drinking tea by candlelight.

He turned around at my approach and watched me, eyes shadowed with concern. A part of me quivered with nervous anticipation as I drew closer, but I rested my gaze on the steaming mug of tea he held in his hands.

'Have you got any more?' I asked, as I halted in the doorway.

Markus nodded and rose to find me another mug. I slid into a chair and thanked him as he placed the mug of tea into my hands. Warmth spread through my body as I held it, and I realised that I was still trembling from the aftermath of my dream. The tea scalded my tongue as I took a sip, and I hastily lowered the mug. Markus didn't say anything, but his forehead creased subtly.

'What are you doing up?' I asked, if only to break the silence. I needed to distract myself if I wanted to keep the memory of the nightmare at bay.

'Keeping watch,' Markus said, 'I only came down here to warm up before going back on deck. The men and I are taking shifts now, after what happened.'

'What time is it?'

'It's early in the morning,' he replied, 'dawn won't be for a few more hours yet. Why are you up?'

'Bad dream,' I muttered, clutching the mug tighter.

'Do you want to talk about it?' I shook my head. Markus sighed, and stood up. 'Well, I'm heading back on deck. You can come along if you want, or you could stay here and enjoy the silence, your choice.'

'I'll come,' I said, and I followed him out the door.

'I'll join you in a minute,' he said, and so I climbed on deck alone, trying not to spill the tea. The night air made me shiver violently, and the cold wind woke me up more effectively than I had expected. I settled myself on a pile of ropes near the edge of the deck and took another fortifying sip of tea. It warmed my whole body, but it didn't stop my violent shivering. I was just at the point of returning to my cabin to warm up when Markus appeared. He was wearing a thick vest which was layered with fur, and he draped a fur-lined blanket around my shoulders. As he sat beside me, I began to warm up, and I was grateful that the blanket protected me from the wind.

'So, it is true,' he broke the silence after a while.

'What is?' I asked, surprised.

'You sleep in that *thing*,' his voice was distasteful as he gestured at my headscarf. I laughed, and reached up to ensure that it was still in place.

'I told you it was practical,' I said, 'why didn't you believe me?'

'Simply because I can see no reason for a young woman to go around with her hair covered by an old scarf,' Markus replied, 'that is if you even have hair.'

'Of course I do,' I spoke automatically.

'I know,' he grinned at my expression, 'your hair's red.'

'How do you know that?' I asked, my defenses rising.

'I found a long red hair beside my bath,' Markus said, 'and since neither I nor Erik have long red hair, and no one else has used my bath of late, that led me to the conclusion that it must be yours.'

My breathing began to return to normal.

'How well-reasoned of you,' I said dryly. 'Did it take a long time to figure it out?'

'All of thirty seconds,' he replied. 'I'm not as slow-witted as you suppose.' He sounded irritated and I grinned. He shifted beside me and his leg pressed against mine. Suddenly all the nerves in my body were on edge and my heart was pounding again, but this time not with fear. Something began gnawing at my stomach and I felt vaguely sick.

'You can see all the stars in the sky from here,' I said, attempting to calm my emotions. I pointed upwards, tracing the constellations with a finger. 'There's the Hanging Rock, Morpheus, the Great Wolf of Summer and …' I trailed off as I looked upwards at the constellation which seemed to resemble a crooked spire.

'The Ice Flame,' Markus finished for me, 'Something I've always wished I could see in the flesh. Legends tell of the magical fire that will only burn during the reign of the rightful ruler. It's said that when a king or queen is crowned, the flame burns bright, and dies when they do. Its embers remain until their successor is crowned, and then the fire will burn again with new life.'

I held my tongue, for I knew all too well what he was talking about. The Ice Flame had been a part of my family for generations, the one thing which refused to recognise the Usurper as the rightful king for as long as I lived. When I died, it would become no more than an ordinary fire, which would never rekindle. That was how the Usurper knew that I was still living, for one only had to look into the glowing embers to know that Wilhelmina Fiordlasher was alive.

'Why have you never been to see it?' I asked, trying to keep my tone casual.

'It's almost impossible to enter the capital now, and Scardia's king has banned any of the public from seeing the throne room since he took power.'

That would explain it, I thought, the Usurper didn't want it well-known that the Ice Flame was still burning, that it was lying dormant in the embers until I returned. He didn't want his rule being undermined in the slightest way, so he prevented the public seeing the one thing which would symbolise his illegitimacy to the throne. Markus glanced sideways at me, 'I would've thought you knew that, considering that you've lived in Scardia longer than I have.'

'Our parents' farm was rather isolated,' I said lamely, after a little pause. 'We didn't have much understanding of what went on in the outside world, and they weren't the kind of people to talk about politics when next season's planting had to be done the next day.'

I hated telling lies. I had gotten so accustomed to telling them over the years, but it still hurt as I spoke words which Markus had no reason not to believe. A part of me shrivelled up inside as I spoke, hating myself for what I had become.

Markus showed no signs of seeing through me, and instead he took the empty mug from my hands and placed it on the deck. I wrapped the blanket more securely around myself as his arm held me closer against his side. He raised his eyebrows as I glanced at him suspiciously.

'It's cold,' he said, 'I'm just ensuring that we don't freeze up here.'

As excuses went it was rather pathetic, but I didn't have the heart to contradict him. Instead, I leaned my head on his shoulder, and relaxed. This felt so nice, perhaps dangerously so. Deep down inside me, a creature purred and demanded that I nestle closer into his warmth. However, another part reminded me that it was pointless and that I couldn't allow myself to be caught up in this fantasy life that I was creating. I couldn't forget my true identity, the dangers connected with it, and the impact it could have on those who were close to me. The instinct to flee and cut myself off from others was strong and deeply ingrained after years of hiding and constant fear of detection. But I was also tired, so tired, of running. All I wanted was to really be Karliah Merryweather, the daughter of two deceased farmers with a younger brother called Erik.

'Do you believe in things like fate and destiny?' I asked quietly, 'that the gods write our tales long before we are born, and we just enact their will? Or can we choose our own tales?'

Markus was silent for a moment, and then said, 'I think the gods are merely things people create to call on in times of need, or to blame when things go wrong.'

He had a point. But how then would he describe the Lord of Spring and the Winter Spirit? I knew that they had powers unknown to man, and if they existed, who was to say that the gods didn't as well?

'And what about people's fate?' I asked, 'are we predestined to follow a certain path, or can we change it?'

'You're very philosophical tonight all of a sudden,' Markus said lightly, and I could hear his smile. 'What brought on this mood, I wonder?'

'Just answer the question,' I said, before adding, 'please.' Markus laughed.

'Of course I don't believe in destiny or fate, I'm the only person who will determine what I do with my life. I won't be someone else's puppet.'

'I envy you,' my voice was bitter. 'It must be wonderful to choose your own fate.'

'Now this is starting to sound familiar.' Markus's hand began to stroke the top of my head and I was surprised at how good it felt. 'You said this earlier, I thought I recognised the *dulcet* tone.' His tone was tinged with sarcasm. 'You certainly believe in these things,' he continued, 'or you wouldn't keep raising them.' He tilted my head up so that I was facing him. In the moonlight his eyes were dark orbs, reflecting the night sky. 'What happened to you and your family was not fated to happen, Karliah. And those mercenaries won't be able to hurt you or Erik again.'

'They'll never stop trying to find me.' The words slipped out before I could hold them back, and from Markus' frown I instantly regretted them.

'I thought they wanted both of you,' he said slowly, 'as payment for your parents' debts.'

'Oh, yes that's right,' I whispered, mortified. How could I have forgotten that part of Erik's story? I felt like a complete idiot, and I hoped that the darkness was hiding the blush that was spreading across my cheeks. 'I don't think they will know where—'

'They're not real are they, Karliah?' His tone was sharp, and he was giving me that scary, impenetrable look. 'Were they just a story to get you passage on a ship leaving Scardia?'

The honest answer was yes, but somehow I didn't think Markus would react well to that, let alone to the fact that most of the things Erik and I had told him about ourselves were also lies.

'No,' I said quietly, 'they weren't a story. Erik might have … exaggerated a little, but…'

'So, there are men chasing you or there aren't?' He still sounded angry, and I froze, staring into his eyes. I couldn't bring myself to lie right now and so I settled for something closer to the truth.

'There are men who are after me,' my voice trembled and I wished it wouldn't, 'they don't care about Erik. They just want me.'

'Why?' His tone was forceful, and I was almost about to tell him, but my common sense stepped in and saved me.

'I can't say,' I whispered, 'please don't ask me to.'

He didn't speak for a long time, but watched me broodingly, lips pressed together in a thin line. And then he looked towards the ocean and resumed stroking my head. I breathed a sigh of relief, relaxed again into his side and closed my eyes. The soft lapping of the waves and the warmth of the blanket were soon enveloping me in peaceful oblivion, and I finally drifted off to sleep, as Markus began humming a quiet lullaby.

Chapter Fifteen

'I believe,' Dylan said over lunch, 'that we should arrive in Lowton this evening. Of course, there'll be no question of finding adequate accommodation then, so I will disembark tomorrow morning. Have you thought about which inn you will stay in?'

I nodded, trying to not respond to Markus's head turning in our direction.

'Very good, very good,' Dylan said approvingly, 'I will be staying at the Crown and Anchor: a very particular establishment which I'm told is highly regarded. But it isn't a place for the everyday rabble to stay, no; its clientele are usually people of much higher calibre.' He puffed out his chest importantly.

'And with larger coin purses, I'm sure,' I said dryly, while mentally reminding myself to not even attempt finding a room at the Crown and Anchor.

'After all, when I tell them that I am Dylan Shorewalker, head scholar to the Lord of Winterdale, I'm sure that they will give me priority treatment,' he continued proudly.

'We'll be going to the lower side of town,' Erik grinned as he caught my eye; obviously he was glad Dylan wouldn't stay near us either, 'but I don't know when we'll head there.'

'Like I said to you, Erik,' Markus said across the table, 'you and your sister can stay as long as you like until you find your family. We will be in Lowton longer now as we will need to have repairs done and find more crew members. And if you stay, I see no need to stop your fencing lessons.'

Erik's grin spread wider, and he positively jumped out of the galley.

'Well, he certainly seems very keen to remain on this vessel,' Dylan sniffed, 'personally I can't wait to be on dry land again. The sea air is very damaging to my manuscripts, and I don't think the spirits like being disrupted by the constant rocking motion of sea travel.'

'But how can spirits feel the boat moving?' I asked. 'Surely they're ethereal beings who aren't able to feel the way that we can?'

'They can feel that the rhythmic vibrations are different,' Dylan said pugnaciously, and I bit the inside of my cheek to refrain from laughing.

'How … unfortunate for them,' I said, amused.

Dylan gave a loud humph of annoyance and strode away, slamming his cabin door with a resounding crash. Now I couldn't hold back the laughter and let it spill out as I began to collect up the dishes.

'You can't seem to get through a single conversation with that man,' Markus commented, 'somehow you always end up annoying each other into storming off.'

'I can't help it if he makes me laugh with his ludicrous ideas,' I replied, 'and I don't mean to annoy him. He's just sensitive.'

'He's a lot more sensitive than anyone else I've met,' Markus agreed, as he too left. Lisette fluttered through the doorway and settled on the back of a chair, preening herself. I paid her no notice as I methodically cleaned up, humming to myself. When I finished, she flew onto my shoulder and nibbled my earlobe, chirping happily. Together we headed to the hold to rub Dolce down.

The sea travel had not been pleasant for Dolce. She had lost weight and was easily startled. She had multiple grazes from hitting the sides of her stall, and she shifted nervously as I approached.

'We'll be off this boat soon, dear one,' I murmured, stretching out my hand to stroke her neck, 'then you can stretch your legs and eat as much grass as your heart desires. You can sleep in a warm stable with fresh hay. You will be able to feel the breeze and see the sun, not just the inside of this ship.' Dolce nickered softly and nuzzled against me, butting Lisette off my shoulder without any apparent regret. Lisette squawked and resettled herself on my other shoulder, shooting Dolce a sharp look.

'But where will we go once we arrive in Lowton?' I mused, 'I can hardly expect to remain here for a long time, it'll be suspicious if no imaginary family shows themselves within the first few days of our arrival. We can't have Markus suspecting any more than he probably already does, after my slip-up last night. And I can't tell Erik; he'll figure out sooner or later that I have next to no idea what to do or where to go.' Lisette ruffled her feathers and chirped encouragingly. It was like she was telling me not to worry, that I would figure something out once we arrived. I wished that I could share her confidence.

'I just don't want to have to lie anymore,' I whispered into Dolce's mane, 'my relationship with everyone is based on lies. No one knows the truth except Keely and he's…' I drifted off, eyes suddenly smarting with tears. Lisette gave a soft chirrup and nibbled my earlobe again. It tickled and I laughed, leaning away from the bird. I picked up the brush and began to rub Dolce down, carefully avoiding the areas where she had hurt herself, which Erik and I had tended to yesterday. She remained perfectly still, flicking her tail from time to time and snorting when I drew near to a tender spot.

'But I don't see how I can find my mother's family without the truth becoming clear,' I said, 'Erik has already begun to suspect that Karliah is just a pseudonym, and that I'm not all I appear.'

Lisette squawked, as if to say that I really shouldn't worry about it, and that I could figure out a way to tell Erik the truth once we were staying in Lowton. Her claws dug into my shoulder reassuringly, and I sighed, struck again by how much Lisette seemed to understand. I had never known any other budgerigars like her, most lived in the lower regions of Scardia where it was slightly warmer. However I was pretty sure that most of them did not show the same amount of uncanny awareness as she did.

'I wonder where you came from, Lisette,' I murmured, brushing her feathers with the tip of my finger. She nibbled it when I paused, and I smiled. 'I'm glad that you're with me, though,' I continued, 'it's almost like a part of Keely's here too. I wish I could tell him…'

Tell him what? How sorry I was for misjudging him? How afraid I was that he'd not live to see the summer? That I wish he hadn't met me, so that he would still be alive, throwing unruly residents out of the inn in Little Fleming? Goodness, my winter in Little Fleming seemed like an age away now. I leaned back against the stall, remembering the first night I'd stepped into that town.

The autumn rain had been cold and driving, a sheet of silver water making it impossible to see more than two feet in front of me. In a daze, I had noticed the glowing lights from the inn up ahead and headed towards them, desperate for anything, from a crust of bread to a bowl of soup. The door was heavy to open, and it was well past the hour when the town's residents frequented the inn. Dolce had thrown a shoe just outside the town, and the grumpy stable master had pointed me towards the only place to stay. Keely had been kneeling, placing a log on the fire, while a grey, mangy cat wound itself, purring around his legs. He'd seemed so intimidating when he stood up that I froze in the doorway, sure that he must be a Tracker.

'Missus,' he called out, 'we've got a customer.'

Mrs Jenkins had bustled in, balancing a tray of empty glasses in her hands. Her hard eyes glanced over me, taking in my bedraggled clothing, the water dripping onto the floor and my half-starved appearance. I hadn't eaten a proper meal in days and my stomach was aching with hunger.

'Can I help you?' She asked brusquely, deciding that if I could be in this state then I didn't have a lot of money to spend on ale. She was right.

'I was wondering if—' I began, and then hunched over as coughs racked through me. Keely rose to his feet, concerned. Mrs Jenkins shot him a glance and he was gone. She put down the tray and led me over to the fireplace, pushing me none too gently into a chair next to it. Keely returned with a steaming mug of tea and I drank it gratefully, clutching it between my ragged, gloved hands.

'We don't give charity here,' Mrs Jenkins said reprovingly, 'at this inn we only accept payment for food and board. There's nothing for you here if you can't pay for it.'

'I can work,' I managed to say between coughs, 'I can do anything you want.'

'You've worked in a bar before?' She was now looking at me closely, mouth pursed.

I nodded. She gave a humph of dissatisfaction.

'Well, I suppose I could use a hand in the bar at night. And maybe after you've had a few decent meals you can earn me money in other ways.' I didn't like the harsh smile that spread across her features, but I lowered my head in what I had hoped was mute acquiescence.

Luckily, I had left before I put on enough weight to find out how Mrs Jenkins had wanted to use me, but it didn't take much to figure out what she had intended. In the ship's hold, I shuddered with relief and clutched the stall to stop myself from sinking down to the ground.

Lisette squawked loudly, and flapped her wings, startling me out of my reverie.

'Karliah?' Erik called, 'are you down there?'

'Yes,' I called back, 'what is it?'

His face appeared in the open doorway, 'it's time for my lesson.' I blinked. Had that much time passed already? How long had I been down here?

'Of course,' I said briskly, and gave Dolce a little treat of sugar before leaving, ushering Erik back towards our cabin. When we reached it, I noticed that he'd already opened the book of Scardian lore and prepared the slate by practicing tracing letters of the alphabet in a line.

'Alright,' I said, kneeling beside him, 'let's have a look at this paragraph. Try copying out this here,' I pointed at the start of the first sentence, 'and then once you know how it's spelt and what letters are in it, try to read it aloud.' He began to trace the letters unevenly, and I made him pause to shift his grip on the stick of chalk.

'Ta-he-ar wah-s oh-ne-ce,' Erik began, his forehead wrinkled in concentration as he followed the line of letters with his finger. I halted him again by putting my hand on his arm. He paused and looked up at me.

'Now, when there are the letters 't' and 'h' next to each other like this,' I said, 'we put them together to make 'th'.' I emphasised the sound, and Erik copied me.

'Th-ear—' he began.

'There,' I corrected.

'Was oh-ne-ce a king,' Erik continued.

'Once,' I interjected, 'keep going.'

'called Ed … Edwa…'

'Edward,' I said patiently, underlining the letters on the page.

'Edward Lightbringer,' Erik finished.

'Well done,' I smiled, 'now read it again.'

And so the afternoon went on, and Lisette and I watched Erik practise to form the words on the slate until it was nearing dusk. At that point, I put away the book and together we went up on deck to watch the Eastern Lands draw closer. We stood next to Dylan who was silent for once, his attention captivated by the town. Erik gazed avidly at the shoreline getting closer and closer, the lights of Lowton twinkling.

I could see the shapes of tall trees and mountains in the distance, beyond the sprawling stone houses of Lowton. Markus shouted out orders and the sailors moved around us, untying ropes and pulling in the sails. At the helm, Markus turned the wheel slowly, edging the ship gradually closer to the dock. We pulled in opposite another ship and immediately sailors threw ropes over the side to moor. There was a loud rattling splash as the anchor was released, and the ship came to a juddering halt. I breathed a sigh of relief, and smiled as the crew laughed, slapping each other on the back companionably.

Markus came down to join us, rubbing his hands together and shooting out orders left and right. He paused in front of us, and my stomach jolted as his eyes met mine.

'The others are going to eat at an inn not far from here,' he said, 'but I'll be staying on board.'

'We can join you,' I said quickly, 'it's a bit too late for us to wander the streets of a town we don't know.' Dylan sniffed at my reply, and said,

'Well don't let *me* intrude on your last night together. I'm going to get a half-decent meal.' With that he strode off, leaving my cheeks stained pink and Markus glancing embarrassed at a floorboard to my left. Erik looked from Markus to me, excitement in his eyes. But Dylan's words struck home, as I realised that this indeed could be our last night on Markus's ship.

'We'll be the only ones here, then,' Markus said with a forced casualness, 'I was thinking of catching some fish and getting some things from a friend when I go to see the harbourmaster.'

'Can I catch fish too?' Erik asked, 'I'm sure I'd be able to catch twice as many. Can I? Can I? Can I?' He pleaded with me and I laughed.

'As long as Markus has no problem with it.'

'None at all,' he said smoothly, 'and I was going to ask the men to get your horse out of the hold before darkness fully sets in. I think it would be best if she was in a proper stable tonight.' I smiled, delighted.

'Thank you,' I said, 'if they have the time that would be most appreciated.'

'They'll find the time,' Markus replied, and began walking away before adding, 'and if you need to take a bath before dinner you can use my cabin. You'll be guaranteed more privacy there.'

'Thank you,' I repeated gratefully. Who knew when I would get to have another bath? And yet I remained on deck for a while, watching as the sailors led Dolce out of the hold and eased her off the boat, disappearing into the twilight. A part of me wanted to go with them to keep her calm, but I knew that it was a lot more dangerous for me to wander these streets at night. Who knew how far the Usurper's influence spread?

From the docks I heard Erik's laughter as Markus showed him the best way to catch a fish with twine and a hook, and I was glad that if only for a short time, Erik could experience life with all of the unknown excitement and mysteries that childhood held.

When the cool air became too chilly for me to bear, I went down below. Lisette followed me as I made my way to the cabin and picked out my only other faded brown dress, clean stockings and underclothes. The dress I was wearing was in dreadful need of a wash and I decided that finding a laverie would be high on my list of priorities for tomorrow. The budgerigar began to sing as we headed to Markus's cabin, which was blissfully empty. I had only just stepped across the threshold when two burly crewmen appeared behind me, carrying steaming buckets of water. They didn't look at me, which I thought was a bit odd, but made two more trips in cool silence before shutting the door behind them. I stared after them, confused. Were they upset that they had to go out of their way to prepare a bath and take my horse to a stable?

A bitter laugh escaped me as I stripped off, imagining how much more they would be expected to do if my true identity was known. Lisette settled on the screen hiding the bath from the doorway and watched as I submerged myself in the hot water. I gasped at the heat and watched as my skin turned as red as my hair in the steam. The headscarf lay next to my dress, and my hair draped across my shoulders, falling in long tendrils to float in the water and scrape the floor.

I sighed and relaxed, stretching out as my stress evaporated like the steam. When the water started to cool down, I reached over and picked up the soap from a nearby table. I scrubbed every inch of my body and washed my hair again, because who could be sure when I would next get the chance to do that?

Lisette was chirping happily to herself, hopping to and fro across the screen in a strange sort of dance. I smiled as I watched her, and rose, dripping from the bath, to wrap myself in a towel. The fire was burning low in the grate, and I dried myself beside it before pulling on my fresh clothes. I wrapped my hair in the towel and knelt to check that I hadn't left any hairs lying around. When I was certain that I had left no traces behind, I picked up my old clothes and padded softly out of the cabin.

Erik was sitting in his hammock, and my nose wrinkled at the smell of dirty water and fish.

'Go and bathe, Erik,' I said bluntly.

'But dinner will nearly be ready,' he objected.

'I'm sure that Markus can hold off cooking for five more minutes,' I said, 'now go and have a bath. When you're clean we'll be able to eat, but not before then.' Grumbling under his breath, Erik left and when the door closed behind him, I pulled my comb out of my chest and began tending to the knots in my hair. My eyes watered as I untangled knot after knot, and I was nervous that at any given moment Erik could walk back in.

It was Lisette who gave me warning of his return, for I could hear her shrill song echoing down towards our cabin. Hastily, I plaited my damp hair and covered it with my headscarf a second before Erik opened the door. Wordlessly, I beckoned for him to come closer and began to pull the comb through his hair ruthlessly. He squirmed and tried to pull away, but I held his shoulder firmly with one hand.

'There,' I said after a few minutes, 'now you're presentable.' He glared at the floor and rubbed his head with a nail-bitten hand, ruffling up the hair that I had just tidied.

'Should we go?' I said, 'I want to see how many fish you caught for dinner.'

This seemed to bolster his spirits and he began telling me about the fish that he had caught, albeit with Markus's help, as we walked towards the galley.

'And then the line started pulling really tight,' he said, 'and Markus said that I'd caught one, so I started to wind it in. I nearly got it out of the water but then the line broke and it got away,' his expression clouded over.

'That's annoying,' I said, 'what did you do then?'

'Markus got another line ready and I reeled in the next fish that came along,' Erik beamed proudly, 'and Markus was going to show me how to gut it, but first he hit it on the head so that it died and stopped jumping around.'

'Really,' I said, 'that's…' But I didn't get the chance to finish my sentence as we reached the galley and were overwhelmed by the smell of cooking fish. Markus was preparing three plates, each one piled with potatoes, peas and a strange charred, yellow vegetable. As I watched, he pulled a charred, oblong vegetable off the stove and cut down its edges, making its yellow peas cascade into a pile, which he divided between the plates. The fish soon followed and he turned, carrying two plates in his hands.

'Have a seat,' he said as he lowered the plates in front of us. 'It's a bit less formal tonight,' he continued as he joined us, 'seeing as Viktor and the others are spending the night in town.'

'That means we have you all to ourselves,' Erik said buoyantly, 'just like last night.'

I blinked as I recalled the early hours of this morning, and the warmth of lying against Markus's shoulder. I looked at my plate, feeling my cheeks redden, and tasted the fish. The slightly charred flesh melted in my mouth and I swallowed it, relishing the taste.

'Did you catch all this fish, Erik?' I asked, 'it's very impressive for your first attempt.'

'I only caught mine,' Erik said proudly, 'Markus said I could only eat what I caught myself. He got the rest. But I helped him pull the lines in and clean the fish.' He grinned, puffing up his chest at his accomplishment.

'I thought that your sister would not appreciate having to catch her own fish,' Markus smiled, and my breathing hitched up a notch when his eyes met mine.

'Thank you,' I murmured, dipping my head to avoid the directness of his gaze.

'What's this?' Erik asked, pointing at the yellow peas on his plate, as he prodded them curiously.

'That's called corn,' Markus replied, 'it grows here in abundance. It's delicious.'

I tasted it and was delighted as a burst of rich sweetness filled my mouth. I let out an appreciative sound and swallowed, smiling as Erik shovelled his own serving down as if it were his last meal on earth. Unlike the night before, all three of us were silent throughout the meal, each enjoying the various flavours.

Only when I was clearing up the plates did I speak.

'Did you get this corn when you went to visit the harbourmaster?'

Markus looked up at me and nodded.

'I had to inform him of our arrival and our expected stay, as well as pay him for mooring here. I also saw fit to ask if he knew of any markets that were still open at a late hour where I could get some fresh ingredients.'

'So you went shopping?' Erik asked, 'but you weren't gone for long?'

Markus laughed, 'thankfully the harbourmaster had some corn which he sold me for a price, seeing as all the shops were long since closed.' He smiled at me, and I couldn't resist smiling back. 'After all,' he continued, his gaze never leaving mine, 'I find that I quite like introducing you to new things.'

It could almost have been as though he was speaking just to me, and my spine shivered at the intimacy in his tone. But then Erik spoke, and the moment between us was broken.

'I like that you've taught me how to fish and fight...'

'And how to wash yourself,' I muttered. Erik grimaced at me.

'She can't teach me any of those things,' he pointed a thumb in my direction as I scrubbed the dishes with a wry smile. 'All she does is tell me off because I can't read properly.'

'I don't tell you off, Erik,' I said calmly, 'I correct you. You've made a great deal of progress since we started on this trip, and I don't think many other boys would have accomplished the same amount while learning other new skills.'

'Really?' He asked, and I could tell that he was pleased with the compliment.

'Of course,' Markus answered, 'I'm pretty sure that you could become anything you put your mind to.'

Erik beamed and began rocking back and forth on his chair. 'I'm going to be a knight one day,' he said. His eyes lit up and he paused for a moment as he wielded an imaginary sword in mid-air. 'I'll be saving people from towers and killing dragons and fighting alongside kings.' He brought the sword down as the chair fell back to the ground with a thump, and mimed stabbing some unknown beast.

I paused, to see how Markus would react. The last thing Erik needed was for the man whom he seemed to idolise to denounce his dearest wish.

'Then a knight you shall be,' Markus said, 'but remember Erik, that knights need to worry about decorum and manners and all manner of toff. Become a sailor instead and you won't have to worry about any of that upper-class nonsense.'

Erik laughed and I joined him as I began to wipe down the dishes and return them to their places. 'Another thing you need to know Erik,' Markus continued, 'if you are to be a knight, is how to dance.' He disappeared for a moment and then returned carrying a gramophone, which he placed on the table. He wound it up and placed the needle down on the record which began to spin.

Music swelled within the galley, and I was transported back in time to another evening when I had watched my parents and other couples waltz around a dance floor. My father had seen me through the banisters and waved me down. In front of the foreign dignitaries and ministers, he began teaching me the steps, and they looked on with either shock or amusement.

I began to hum along with the tune, and swayed with the beat as I returned the final plate to the cupboard.

'You know this one?' Markus asked, surprised.

'Of course,' I answered automatically, 'the King's Waltz.'

'Then perhaps you should teach your brother the steps,' he said. 'If he aims to associate with nobility, he needs to know how to dance.'

I held out my arms to Erik who approached me tentatively, obviously unsure if dancing was as masculine as swordplay or fishing. I placed his arm on my waist and mine on his shoulder, and began to count: one, two, three, close. One, two, three, close. After a few missteps, he seemed to get the hang of it, although he was still quite stiff and uncomfortable. The music faltered and died.

There was a tap on his shoulder and Markus cut in.

'Let me show you how it's done, Erik. Watch and learn.' He indicated for the boy to move away, and Erik leapt onto the table and wound the gramophone so that the music began again. Markus's eyes met mine, and he bowed low.

'May I have this dance, milady?'

Oh, how many times I had dreamt about being asked that at my first ball.

I curtsied low and bowed my head. 'You may, milord.' He needed no more invitation but pulled me into his arms, and began to lead, sweeping us around and around the galley in tight circles. I relaxed and moved seamlessly, the muscle memory from all those years ago kicking in as though it had only been mere hours since my father had last danced with me. It was as though we were floating, kept aloft by the music and the steps, and nothing mattered but the strong hands that held me and the eyes that gazed into mine. As the music deepened in a crescendo, I began to incorporate the intricacies of the dance, the side steps, twirls and pauses, which Markus took in his stride. The climax of the song shattered, and he lifted me high into the air, before dipping me until my hair almost came out of my headscarf to touch the ground.

Erik was watching us, wide eyed.

'I have to learn to dance like that?' He sounded almost scared.

'You can learn the basic steps and then work on them when you're older,' Markus smiled, his gaze not leaving mine, 'and when you find the right partner, you might enjoy it a lot more.' Erik gave a disgusted noise as Markus lifted me back onto my feet.

'Thank you,' I murmured, curtseying again, and he brushed his lips over my knuckles in response. The touch held me mesmerised for a moment, for it made other feelings trickle through me. Erik yawned pointedly and leapt down from the table.

'Well, I suppose that's a clear indicator to say goodnight,' I said with an attempted smile. 'Come along, Erik.' I felt a twinge of sadness: I didn't want the night to end yet.

With a lot of moaning and complaining that he wasn't tired, Erik finally said a disgruntled goodnight to Markus and led the way to the cabin. However, within moments of rolling into his hammock, he was fast asleep. I envied that he could fall asleep so quickly, a feat which I could only accomplish when I was exhausted.

Lisette fluttered next to me and chirped softly, as if to say: if you want to have time alone, now is the time to take it. I didn't need telling twice. A second later I was shutting the door quietly behind me and heading back to the galley. It was empty.

I halted for a moment and then headed for the deck, thinking that I could watch the lights in Lowton a bit longer before turning in. When I reached the deck, I was alone, and I leaned against part of the railing that hadn't been knocked off by the monster. The lights in Lowton were fading now, as people blew out their candles and retired to bed. There were footsteps behind me, and a dark presence appeared at my elbow.

'It's cold out here,' he said gruffly.

Was it? I had barely noticed.

'You should go below,' he continued, but made no move to urge me away. I didn't move.

'I wondered what it would be like when I finally got here,' I said quietly, 'but now that we're here, I'm not sure what to do.' He shifted at my words, but I kept my gaze fixed on the rowdy inn which was at the other end of the wharf. I was sure that the other sailors were inside, celebrating after their time at sea. I wondered if Markus ever joined them on these nights out.

'You can choose,' his voice was as low as mine, and I glanced at him, surprised. His gaze was also fixated on the light filled windows from which laughter and loud voices emerged, their sound travelling to us easily over the silent waters.

'What do you mean?' I asked, my heart suddenly in my throat. He stepped closer,

'I don't want you to leave.' His voice trembled, and I realised that he was probably just as scared as I was.

'Why should you care?' The words left my mouth before I could help myself and old thoughts began filling my head. I was bad luck, no good, a danger to anyone and everyone. He froze and, for a moment, I believed that he would turn and leave. The thought was enough to tear my heart in two. In all my recent dreams I'd envisioned a world where Markus and I could be together. Each dream had been crazier and less likely than the last. If what Rakael and the Winter Spirit had spoken was true, and that there was a resistance growing, then Markus would discover who I was when I sought them out. And I was certain that that knowledge would estrange us forever.

My thoughts shattered in a million pieces as Markus's warm breath touched my ear.

'As if you don't know, farm girl,' he breathed. I stood, paralysed, and full of new tension. What was he doing? Didn't he realise that I was bad news? That, if we were discovered and I was recognised, my presence could get him killed? Of course not, I admonished myself. He believed my name to be Karliah, a farmer's daughter.

'Karliah?'

That name was false. Not me. How I longed to tell him, to hear him call me 'Nina' instead.

'I … I…' All I could manage was a stammer. He was close, too close.

'If you won't stay, let me go with you,' he said, 'I barely trust Erik or that scholar to look after you. I met him as he came back on board and he said that you would both be departing tomorrow.'

'What?' I asked, stupefied. 'Dylan? He's not going anywhere with me, do you think that I could put up with him for one more…' He laughed, cutting me off.

'You can choose your own destiny, Karliah.'

But I couldn't. Not really. 'I can't,' I said lamely, but Markus continued as if I hadn't spoken.

'And I don't think that Erik will be able to look after you, who knows what will happen if your family can't be found. Or if they have other intentions for you once they know that you could be married off, you might find yourself…'

'If you think I'm going to give my heart to someone else, then you're wrong.' I realised, too late, that I had spoken my inner thoughts aloud. Mortified, I turned away, hoping that the dark night would hide the flush that spread across my face and neck. I was all too aware of everything around us: the quiet splash as the water hit the dock, the distant hoot of an owl and the faint sound of Dylan's godforsaken music – or as he believed – his direct connection to the spirits of nature. I only hoped that they were deaf. At that moment I wished that I was too, or that a hole would open in the deck and swallow me whole.

A rough, calloused hand clasped mine, whirling me around, until I was an inch away from Markus's face, from his lips. My own were dry and chapped from the days at sea. Unconsciously my tongue slid over them, moistening them.

'You are impossible,' he whispered, 'I don't understand you at all. You keep surprising me.'

'I can't, I'm not safe …' Oh gods, why was I blabbering? His kiss silenced me, cutting off my measly sentence, lips moving ever so softly against mine.

'Choose this,' he murmured. In that moment time seemed to stand still, as his hands pulled me closer and I clung to him in return. The kiss became more passionate, a blending of tongues and pleasure. I could barely think, let alone speak, for all the emotions and feelings which spiralled through me. His kiss on my hand the other night had only given me a brief idea of what he could make me feel, but this was something entirely new and intoxicating. It was at that moment that I dropped all my defences and resistance, and wound my hands in his hair, holding him closer. After all, who knew how much time we would spend together after tonight?

I was hardly aware of him lifting me up and carrying me down to his dark cabin, closing the door with one foot and laying me down on his bed. Our hands became as desperate as our kisses, tearing at snagging buttons as they pulled our clothing away. All that mattered was this new, fiery desire that raged between us. My hands explored his body with fascination as his lips tasted mine. I felt a brief pain, which was followed by a glowing rush and a blissful release that left us both lying sated in each other's arms. Neither of us spoke or moved, each wanting to prolong the moment for as long as possible. His hand began to stroke down my back, and I shivered although I wasn't cold.

'Where did you learn to dance?' He asked, 'I've never seen steps like you danced tonight.'

'My father taught me,' I replied.

'An odd thing for a farmer to teach his daughter,' Markus mused, forehead crinkled in thought. I raised myself onto my elbows and looked at his silhouette in the darkness, wondering how I would bring myself to leave him now. And yet, come morning I would have to say goodbye. It was inevitable.

My hair had come out of its plait and cloaked my back. I sent out a silent prayer of thanks to the gods for the darkness which shrouded the obvious streak of white. It would be wiser if Markus didn't know that my blood was connected to the Ice Flame. He reached up and wound his fingers in it, following it all the way down to the ends.

'So you don't wear that scarf all the time, then,' he said, and I could've sworn that he smiled.

'Not all the time no,' I said, 'but it is…'

'Practical, I know. Hold on a moment,' he rose from the bed and crossed to the table where he picked up something, before lying back alongside me. 'Sit up,' he ordered, and I obeyed. His rough hands pulled my hair around to the side and I felt something slide around my neck and fall heavily against my collarbone. 'I want you to have this,' he murmured against my head, as he tied the cords together. 'I got it on my first voyage after my parents died. It always seemed to bring luck on every trip. I hope it will bring you luck when I'm not around.' My hair fell back down and I touched the necklace, feeling a small coin against my skin.

'Do you intend to stick around then?' I asked, as I leaned back down onto my elbows.

He chuckled, 'Perhaps, or perhaps you will choose to stay with me.' I smiled, choosing to put aside all thoughts of realistic options for a bit longer.

'Markus?'

'Yeah?'

There was no point in not enjoying myself while I had the chance. 'Take me again.'

His chuckle surprised me, but then all thoughts disappeared as he rolled above me and fulfilled my wish with sweet tenderness. Finally, much later in the night, I fell asleep in his arms, my head resting on his bare chest. I dreamed of a world in which I really was Karliah Merryweather, and chose to stay with him, adventuring the high seas and carrying exotic cargos back and forth across the map. I dreamed that I could sleep beside him every night and wake up to kiss him in the morning. And, mainly, I dreamed that I wasn't Wilhelmina Fiordlasher, the lost princess of the realm, whose destiny had been predetermined many long years ago and who couldn't afford to lose her heart to a ship's captain.

Chapter Sixteen

I awoke slowly, languorously, stretching out in the bed and revelling in the feeling of a soft mattress and sheets instead of a hammock. Markus was breathing deeply next to me, and I sat up, awareness of my surroundings and memories of last night filled my mind. His arm had been holding me and slipped down to rest around my waist as I looked down at him. There was a long tattoo which stretched down his side, winding around and around, spreading across one shoulder and down to the wrist. I had a strong impulse to trace it with my fingers, examine the intricate patterns and kiss the spots where his skin was bare. However the dawn light filtered through the windows, and suddenly I felt terror wash through me. I had to cover my hair as soon as possible.

I slid from the bed sheets and began pulling on my clothing with shaking hands. What had I done? I'd never been this reckless before, and it scared me how I had succumbed, losing myself and my usual defensiveness for one night. But at the same time there was a glowing joy that filled my chest, and I couldn't stop the smile from spreading across my face.

My hands deftly pulled my hair up and back, twisting it around and around before tying the scarf in place. I tiptoed out of the cabin and headed towards my own, wondering what Markus would say when he awoke and found me gone. But I had to return to my cabin before Erik awoke and began asking questions about where I'd been all night. As I opened my door, I breathed a sigh of relief as Erik rolled over in his sleep. Only Lisette was there to see me lie down in my own hammock, and the look in her eyes was disapproving.

'You implied I should enjoy my time with him,' I whispered, 'and I did.'

She chirped, disgusted, and fluttered away, leaving me to grin up at the ceiling like an idiot. I closed my eyes and felt him touch me again, my body responded to the memory and my heart pounded as I remembered every intimate detail of the night before. There was no way that I could sleep anymore, and so I just waited for Erik to awake, caught up in my thoughts. My fingers played with the copper coin around my neck, which flashed in the light. The sun rose higher and Erik awoke, muttering something about dragons and broadswords.

He brought me a slice of bread and cheese for breakfast which I appreciated, the nausea which had often visited me in the past suddenly returning with a vengeance. I forced myself to eat under his anxious gaze, and then together we headed to the deck to watch Lowton come bustling to life. Lisette settled on my shoulder, apparently forgiving me for my earlier indiscretion.

'We should think about finding accommodation in the next few days,' I said, 'we can't intrude on the ship for too long.'

'But Markus said that we could stay as long as we wanted,' Erik said with a slight frown.

'I know he did,' I replied heavily, 'we don't have to leave right away.'

There were footsteps behind us and we turned to face Markus, who nodded at us brusquely. 'Good morning,' he said, without the slightest trace of emotion. I began to feel cold, was he angry? Had he been offended that I had left him before he awoke?

'Good morning,' Erik said, 'can we go fishing again today, Markus? I swear I'll catch more this time.'

'Not right now,' Markus's eyes were on me, 'first I need a word with your sister.' He turned and stalked off, and I followed, suddenly nervous. He was acting like he had before, when I'd been an unwanted passenger on board the ship.

'What's wrong?' I asked tentatively, as he halted in his cabin and faced me, arms folded and expression inscrutable.

'I've been thinking about your payment for the trip,' he began, and I blinked, confused. There was something odd going on.

'Oh, of course,' I said, 'I can get the money now if you wa…'

'You don't have to pay me,' Markus said coldly, and at his tone my soul began to tear into shreds. 'You already paid enough, and adequately, for services rendered.'

My hand flew out, marking his cheek red, and Lisette added to it by biting his earlobe savagely. I was shocked and confused, what had happened to make him change so drastically? His dark eyes stared clearly into mine, unabashed, and I felt tightness constrict my throat. My stomach was an iron-bound chest, filled with leaded weight and sinking to the bottom of the Kraken's Mouth.

'You can't mean that,' I whispered, biting back tears.

'Go,' he said, and I trembled at the hardness in his voice, 'Leave.'

What had happened after last night? What had made him no longer want me to stay, or want to go with me? Had it all been a façade, a lie, just so that he could be repaid for his efforts in the way which Dylan had implied?

Lisette flew off with a screech and I left, too shocked and hurt to scream at him, to demand that he explained his sudden change of heart. I was barely aware of grabbing the few belongings in my cabin and leading Erik by the hand, dragging him off the ship, ignoring his questions or the tears which streaked my cheeks.

I didn't know where we were going and I didn't care. We walked for over an hour, Erik trudging behind me in disgruntled silence. I had only spoken once, to tell him that we weren't going back to that ship now or ever, and I didn't want to hear anything else about it. The cobbled street stretched ahead of us and merged with others, until I was completely lost. Lisette had disappeared and I found that I missed the comforting weight of her on my shoulder. We passed a market where short men shouted out their wares, and people bustled through the tightly packed stalls, balancing their purchases on donkeys. The sweet smell of spices and incense filled my nostrils, and I bought a bag of toasted sugared nuts for Erik, who had been complaining of being hungry for a long time.

My gaze was caught by the glittering ornaments and coloured silks on the next stall and felt a pang of desire to buy myself something beautiful. I squashed the notion and turned away, remembering treacherously the multiple baubles and dresses that had been lavished on me in earlier years. We walked on, and the sun rose higher and began its descent across the sky. Erik munched contentedly on the nuts, and asked what we were going to do and where we would stay the night.

'There,' I said finally, pointing at an inn which was up ahead. We pushed our way through afternoon shoppers and trundling carts towards the doorway. Inside it was cool and quiet, and I approached the innkeeper who was cleaning glasses behind the bar.

'Have you got any rooms free for the night?' I asked, rummaging through my bag to find my coin purse.

'Just one, for ten silver pieces,' he said, smiling at Erik and me. I counted out ten silver coins and he handed over a brass key. 'The second door on the left, up the stairs,' he said, and we nodded our thanks. 'The bathroom is at the end of the hall and we serve dinner from six,' he called after us as we climbed towards our room.

'He seemed nice,' I said encouragingly, as we opened the door to see two pallets lying on the ground near a dirty window. On the other side of the room were a couple of threadbare chairs and an empty hearth. I dumped my bag on the ground and opened the grimy panes. Erik sank down onto his pallet and stared at me.

'What do we do now?' he asked.

Outside the window, tall stately trees rose upwards, their trunks white and smooth, their leaves forming a canopy high above. They stretched back as far as the eye could see, with wildflowers and high grasses forming a carpet beneath them. Birds swooped amongst the branches, splashes of bright colour against the sea of green.

'Karliah?' Erik sounded impatient.

'I need to find my family,' I said quietly, 'and find out where Dolce is.' I couldn't believe that I had forgotten about her until now, and my stomach twinged with shame.

'She was taken to one of the bigger stables in the city,' Erik said, 'I heard some of the crew talking about it last night. She'll be alright; we just have to find a map or something to know how to find her.'

I smiled, 'what a good idea.' My throat was still tight, as it had been all day, and the tears that I had shed earlier were threatening to fall again. I turned back to the window, hoping that Erik hadn't seen the tears. To my surprise, he rose and gave me a brief hug, which I returned with one arm. There was a loud chirp and a ball of yellow and green feathers landed on the windowsill.

'Lisette,' I exclaimed, picking the bird up in my hands, 'I wondered where you went.'

Erik rubbed her back with his thumb and then headed to the doorway, 'I'm going to ask the innkeeper if he has a map.'

I nodded and sat down to remove my shoes, my legs aching after walking all day. My feet were red and blistered and I ached to bathe them in cold water. Before I could get up to walk to the bathroom, Erik returned with a pile of papers which scattered across the floor as he sat down.

'He said that there are three major stables in Lowton, and that they are here, here and here,' he pointed at circled dots on the map, 'and we are all the way over here.' He indicated another dot on the other side of the map, 'So tomorrow we should go to the nearest stable and see if we can find her.'

'It does give us something to do for the next few days,' I admitted, 'and I *would* feel better knowing where Dolce is.' That was an understatement; without the horse nearby I felt as though a part of me was missing. To make things worse I was still smarting over what Markus had said earlier. My mind was numb, while my body ached and stung from the blisters, and I was unaware of time passing. Erik's words as he pored over the map faded into background noise, and I couldn't summon any more interest than I had previously expressed. I only murmured the correct pronunciation of street names when he had difficulty with them, but otherwise I gazed back out of the window at the forest beyond.

I wondered vaguely what my father had felt when he first arrived here, in the company of his father and courtiers, knowing that his marriage was preordained and necessary to save his kingdom and crown. In the times my parents had retold the tale, his eyes had misted over as he described the Eastern Lands and the home of my mother's people. I only wished that he had explained how exactly he had found them.

Erik was silent and subdued that evening, preferring to stay on his pallet than to practise writing his letters in the dust around the hearth with me. I had calmed down a lot more after bathing my tender feet, and it seemed that as I got more talkative, he had become less so. I tried not to let it get to me, I knew that he was secretly disappointed that Markus hadn't come with us. When I said, with a painful ease over dinner, that it had only been his job to ferry us across the Meridian, Erik had looked at me directly and I realised that he knew. Maybe not about my fall from grace, but at least that something drastic had happened between Markus and I, and that things between us wouldn't be the same again.

I had known that this separation would be inevitable and difficult, but I hadn't expected to leave on such painful terms. My brain still couldn't process how it had happened, what he'd said, what I'd done. Markus's actions this morning had been so different and confusing that I kept going over what could have changed his feelings so abruptly. Lisette was feasting on some seeds in my palm and, sensing the turn of my thoughts, looked up at me beadily as if to say, 'you brought this on yourself, you know.'

I was still wearing the copper coin necklace that he had given me. He had said it would bring me luck. Why then did I feel as though all of my luck had dried up? I rubbed it absentmindedly, slowly watching my reflection get clearer. Whoever was next door to us was making a lot of noise; there were the sound of thuds and chairs being overturned. But after Dylan I was used to loud neighbours and didn't mind as much as I might have done.

Suddenly there was a loud banging on the door. I looked up, my heart in my throat and thoughts flitting through my mind. Was it Markus? Had he found us to make amends? Erik looked at me as he moved to the door and I nodded. I gasped as he was nearly bowled over as the door burst open.

'By what right, madam,' an annoyingly familiar voice declared, 'do you have to take my Sigilium Opiatus?'

Erik glared up at the speaker as I brushed the dust off my skirt and rose to my feet.

'And by what right sir,' I said calmly, 'do you barge into my room and accuse my brother and I of something we are innocent of doing?'

Dylan Shorewalker stared at me for an instant, his eyes bulging behind his monocle, mouth opening and closing stupidly for a few seconds.

'You took my Sigilium Opiatus,' he stated again, but this time he sounded childish and uncertain. 'You took it from my cabin last night!'

'And *what* is a Sigilium Opiatus?' I asked coldly.

'It is an important fragment of my Opium Sigilus manuscript, which is of infinite value, as it discusses the powers of the Sigilium stones that the ancient inhabitants of Scardia used. It's a major aspect of my research and will let me explain to the Lord of Winterdale about our country's special history.'

I looked at Dylan, unimpressed. How could he be so completely caught up in the days of the ancient past and their artefacts, instead of the issues of the present? I was pretty sure that this Lord of Winterdale was as uninterested as I was, and it was for this reason that he had sent this man on a journey to the Eastern Lands.

But you don't stand up against these issues either, that treacherous voice in my mind whispered. You, who keeps running and hiding and jumping at shadows.

'Let me get this straight,' I said slowly, 'you believe that we stole some old piece of a manuscript from your cabin?' Dylan nodded emphatically, his monocle wobbling. 'My brother is learning to read,' I said angrily, 'and I have no interest whatsoever in ancient manuscripts. It seems that you have misplaced this Sigilium Opiatus by yourself and just want to blame someone else for your own incompetence.' Lisette squawked in agreement.

For a moment Dylan seemed lost for words, and in that instant I glanced at Erik, frowning when he didn't meet my gaze. Dylan followed my glance and pounced.

'You, boy, you know something don't you? Tell me! You came into my cabin, didn't you? You saw my Sigilium Opiatus and thought you'd earn yourself a pretty penny, didn't you, you scrawny thief?'

'How dare you!' I cried, stepping forward to shield Erik from him. The boy quivered behind me, and I was reminded of the first time I had seen him. 'My brother is not a thief.'

'You were the only other passengers!' He positively screeched, eyes wide and demented, 'and the manuscript isn't amongst the rest of my translations, nor my other belongings! It was there last night and now it's gone!'

'Maybe you should learn to look more thoroughly,' I said coolly, 'we have no need for manuscripts or gold.'

'You lie!' Dylan's face was transcendent with rage, and I felt fear wash through me as he stepped closer, fists clenching. For a moment I thought that he was going to hit me.

Thankfully I was wrong. As he drew closer, Lisette gave a loud shriek and flapped around his head, before landing on my shoulder again. In such close proximity with the budgerigar, Dylan covered his face with his hands and a high-pitched whimpering filled the room. It took me a moment to realise that he was the source, and I laughed. Erik joined me and together we moved away.

When he realised that he wasn't in any danger from Lisette, Dylan glared at us balefully. 'You'll regret stealing from me,' he spat, 'you're nothing, you worthless little…' He cut off, his eyes growing wide as he stared at something behind us.

Before I could turn around three things happened.

Erik cried out in fear, a memory of Markus - his eyes cold and hard, bearing the mark of my hand across his cheek without shame - flashed before my eyes, the world went black, and I knew no more.

I awoke on a bed that felt lighter than a spider's web. Pale dawn light was drifting down through the roof above me. I blinked and slowly sat up, rubbing a sore spot on the back of my head. On closer inspection, the ceiling seemed to be made of twisted branches, almost like wicker work, but with leaves and vines and bell-shaped flowers thrown in. It was incredible. As if in a dream, I got to my feet and padded across the floorboards towards a doorway. Instead of a door, feathers, bells, and leaves hung down on thin strings. I turned back to look at the bed and admired its woven headboard, which twisted upward to the ceiling. Thin gossamer sheets lay crumpled where I had been lying, and I went back and smoothed them. When the bed looked as neat as I could make it, I pushed aside the strings in the doorway, and as I walked down a wide hallway the air was filled with a pleasant tinkling. The hallway widened out into a large platform, which I realised must be in the canopy of the trees. At this level, they were packed so tightly and spread so far that I couldn't see the faintest glimmer of the Meridian. Where was I?

'So, you're awake at last.' I spun around and found myself face to face with an old man who was sitting on a carved wooden chair. No, not a chair. A throne.

'Do you know who I am, child?'

I shook my head, still dazed and disorientated by my surroundings.

'A pity,' he said, and then waved a hand. As if on cue, Erik and Dylan appeared between two silent, armoured figures. I drank in the sight of my adopted brother, relief coursing through my veins that he appeared safe and unhurt. He was gazing around in wonder, while Dylan was looking grumpy. 'As you can see,' the man continued, 'we haven't harmed your … friends.'

'Why am I here?' Dylan cried, 'I demand to be returned to the inn immediately. You can't keep me here against my will! I won't allow it! How did we get here? I demand to be let go!'

'In that case, you can take the boy with you,' the man said calmly.

'No!' Erik said loudly, at the same time as Dylan spluttered,

'But he's her brother!'

At this comment the old man laughed. 'She has no brother,' he declared, and I felt myself go cold. He looked at me, and I was struck by his pale blue eyes. Something inside me was crying out, celebrating, dancing in happy circles as I stepped towards him, still gazing into those eyes. I couldn't speak; terrified by the hope that was rushing up which I hadn't felt for years.

'Yes, he is,' Dylan said, confused. Erik was silent, and I could feel that he was watching me as intently as I was the old man.

'He is no more of her blood than he is of yours.' The man said, 'besides Wilhelmina Fiordlasher is an only child.'

There was complete silence, and then Dylan burst out laughing. I turned and saw him clutch his sides, the monocle falling down on its chain to swing aimlessly. Erik was staring at me wide-eyed, comprehension dawning in his gaze.

'That's preposterous!' Dylan gasped, 'she isn't the princess. The princess died years ago. And who are you to say who she is?'

The man stood up, and he stood at least a head higher than everyone present. The guards knelt in his presence, and I lowered into a curtsey, recognising that I could no longer hide and should remember my manners. My hand rose to my forehead, mimicking the gesture my father had demonstrated years before, when he first entered the Elven court.

'Her grandfather,' the old man replied, as he took my chin in his hands and lifted it, until I stood as tall as he was. His eyes blazed with icy fire as he looked over me, 'come my child, let's get you into something befitting who you truly are.'

There was no time to talk to Erik or ask him if he was alright. I glanced back as we left the platform and he waved at me and smiled, so I felt slightly better, hoping that we would have time to talk later. The sound of Dylan's spluttering disbelief followed us as my grandfather led me down various hallways, and I swallowed a grin.

'You have interesting travelling companions, Wilhelmina,' he said, as he guided me across a narrow bridge, crossing a hundred-foot drop. 'The boy I have no objection to, he seems to care for you greatly and was most insistent that he knew where you were. That man on the other hand…'

'He wasn't meant to be with me,' I interrupted, 'it was purely accidental that he was there.'

'I sent my men to retrieve you once I knew that you had arrived,' my grandfather continued, 'I had expected you to be travelling alone, but I'm sure that things can be arranged for them to stay with us for a while. They know who you are, and we cannot risk anyone else discovering your location. Time is of the essence these days.'

'I'm sure that Erik will enjoy being here for some time,' I said breathlessly as I tried to keep up with him, 'as for Dylan, he seems pretty set in his decision to return to Lowton.'

'We'll see,' my grandfather said, as he led me into a sun-speckled room where women were gathered around a deep pool. 'I will leave you here until you are ready for luncheon. Giselle will lead you to the dining area when you're ready.' He indicated a willowy woman with pale hair and piercing brown eyes. At his arrival, they had all lowered to the ground, bowing their heads and pressing two fingers against their foreheads. I stared at them awestruck as my grandfather left, and they rose and flocked around me. I felt as though I was a flame and they moths, for they admired me and undressed me with a rapidity that left me feeling awkward. My headscarf and clothing were carried off and I was led into the pool of water, which bubbled invitingly. My blistered feet seared with pain, and I gasped.

'You can relax now, your highness,' Giselle said as another woman leaned over the water, sprinkling in herbs and salts, murmuring words that I couldn't distinguish. One pushed her hair back and I noticed her ears, which reached sharp points. I gazed around the room, watching as the warm light filtered through the leafy canopy and the water sent bright reflections dancing on the floorboards. It was even more incredible than my father had described. I lathered the soap over my body and grimaced as I touched my feet.

'You have been hurt, milady,' Giselle said, 'we can heal you, make you whole again.' Her hands hovered over my feet and then pointed upward towards my abdomen. Her gaze was intent as it met mine as she continued, 'you have been hurt in several ways, milady.' My eyes widened as I understood her meaning. I opened my mouth in shock, stuttering,

'You mean … you can make me…'

'It will be wiser if you ascend Scardia's throne as a virginal queen,' she said quietly, 'no one will know what happened, and you will be pure and whole once more. Historically, being chaste is a powerful means to gather respect and support from those in power. That will be useful when you become queen.' I watched her nervously. I didn't know much about those particular rules of state, my parents hadn't seen the need to explain chastity and the rules and regulations behind ascending the throne to a seven-year-old child. Giselle was watching me, her expression non-judgemental, and the words escaped me before I could think of a proper response to her recommendation.

'Will it hurt?'

Giselle gave a tinkling laugh, 'no more than feeling the brush of a butterfly's wing.'

'Alright,' I said, my mouth dry. I might become whole again, but I wouldn't forget Markus's arms around me or what we had done. That would always remain firmly imprinted in my heart as a night of joy, not the horrible pain that he had caused the next morning.

The elves spoke in unison, some chanting, some singing, and their voices rose in a crescendo before dimming down to a low hum. I didn't understand the words they spoke, but my skin tingled and I felt warmth spread through me, from the roots of my hair to the tip of my toes. They stopped speaking and indicated that I should get out.

As I arose from the bath, I noticed with shock that my skin was clearer, my feet completely healed, my nails long and polished. I felt and looked better than I had in years. I was draped in a soft towel and rubbed down, a soft dress was pulled over my head and fell down to the ground, clinging against my skin. My hair was left loose, and pale slippers were brought forth for my feet.

'Shall we go to lunch?' Giselle asked kindly, and I stammered out my thanks as she led me out of the room. There was a warm breeze, and my hair dried quickly as we crossed bridges and reached another platform, which held a long wooden table that was covered with platters of food. Giselle curtsied to me and bid me farewell, before disappearing, leaving me to approach the table alone.

My grandfather rose from his seat at the head, and Erik followed suit, as did the half dozen other people sitting there. The only one who didn't move was Dylan, who was gawking at me and I felt uncomfortable, shifting uneasily from foot to foot.

'Come, Wilhelmina,' my grandfather said, indicating a chair directly on his right. I settled next to him and gazed down the table. Erik was smiling at me, and I felt relieved that my true identity hadn't seemed to upset him. Dylan's stare had become almost rude, and I turned away to face the white-haired man on my left. 'Let me introduce some of my friends, Ulthor, Graecius, Mayflower, Pierce and Clementine.' He nodded to each of the elves in turn, who bowed before sitting down.

There was one other person who had also sat down, and I felt a strange sense of recognition although I would've sworn that I hadn't seen her before. Her eyes glinted as they watched me, her mouth twisted in a sardonic smile. Dark hair was pulled away from her face in a severe bun, and her dress had a high collar which emphasised the scars that marred her right cheek, spreading from underneath her eye to her chin. It was almost as though she had been mauled by some creature, and I froze as she spoke.

'I believe that we have already met,' her voice was raspy and grating, and suddenly I remembered that we had met before.

'Isabel,' I said, before correcting myself as I remembered what Keely had told me, 'I mean … Rakael.' She inclined her head.

'I see that Keely is not with you.' Her tone was harsh, and I could feel her unspoken judgement, denouncing me for not being able to save him, blaming me for his loss.

'Trackers caught him,' I said through numb lips, 'he told me to run.'

'And so you did,' her voice was expressionless. 'But you are here now, which I suppose is progress.'

'I thought the rebels had a stronghold in the west,' I said.

'We do,' she said, 'but our main base is here. King Aegis,' she inclined her head in my grandfather's direction, 'was so kind as to offer us his protection after our last stronghold was razed by the Usurper.'

He nodded, as the others began to help themselves to the delicacies before them. I served myself, spooning lumps of buttered corn and green leafy vegetables onto my plate. My grandfather piled some finely cut meat next to it, and I thanked him quietly, unsure how to act around him.

'I believe that we are awaiting one more guest, who I'm sure will be most pleased to see you,' he said, and my eyes widened in surprise as Lisette fluttered down onto the ground next to us.

'Lisette,' I began to reach down, but my grandfather clicked his fingers and muttered something, and Lisette was gone. In her place was a short woman with curly blonde hair and beady eyes that smiled into mine. I stared, shocked, and I heard Dylan say,

'Good heavens … that bird was … but she's a … what in the blazes is going on here?'

She curtsied and took her place next to one of the elves, and didn't speak a word as they served her.

'She's mute,' my grandfather said at my confused expression, 'but she proves herself useful in other ways. She was able to communicate which inn you were staying in, which was vital for us to find you. I gather that she thinks rather highly of you.' His eyes perused Lisette's serene expression, 'and I'm sure that she will be pleased to tend to you as a handmaiden.'

'I don't need a maid,' I said quickly, 'I can take care of myself.'

'Indeed you can.' His tone was dry as conversation around the table restarted, 'I would have expected you to come much sooner. I was almost sharing the belief of many others that you had died.'

'I didn't know where to go,' I said, 'and I was sure for a long time that the Usurper would expect me to go to the Eastern Lands. I'd never met you before, and I didn't know if I would be welcome.' I looked down at my plate, suddenly ashamed. If I had come here years ago, I would have been spared so much pain and fear, I wouldn't have known the harshness of cold winter nights or the pain of hunger. But then I wouldn't have met Keely, Erik, Markus … I blinked at the thought and resolutely focussed my attention on my grandfather's next words.

'Your mother wanted to bring you here,' he said softly, 'she wrote to me before that dreadful night, telling me about her suspicions that something was amiss. Unfortunately, the ship she had planned to use was never boarded, and you disappeared. My daughter died and my granddaughter was gone.'

'Why did you never come looking for me?' I asked.

'If I had acted so rashly Lord Niall would have waged war against my people. We had already lost so many from the previous wars and the wounds were still fresh in my people's minds. I could not ask them to do that again, especially if you had died. Instead, I heightened security, and hoped that you would find your own way here.'

'Were sea creatures part of this new security?' I asked, my mouth dry as realisation began to dawn.

'Yes,' he replied, 'Alexia was most pleased to inform me of your imminent arrival.'

'Alexia?'

'She's a very … special creature,' he said, smiling, 'but she bows to my will, which is all that matters.'

I couldn't speak for a moment. That monstrous creature with the seven frilled heads and long teeth had a *name*? And my grandfather spoke about it as he would a pet, with tender appreciation.

'That creature nearly killed us,' I said.

'Not when she knew who was on board,' my grandfather corrected me. I remembered how the creature had stared at me, and then leapt away through the waves. It was starting to make sense.

'But she killed people,' I reinforced, 'innocent people.'

He raised his eyebrows at me, 'just because she obeys me doesn't mean that she can help her nature. She only interferes with incoming vessels, and this one had strange noises coming from it, or so she told me.'

'What do you mean by strange noises?' I looked over at Dylan, wondering if he had been communicating with the spirits before the monster came. Maybe sea creatures had even less tolerance for his rain stick and chanting than I did.

He shrugged, 'something that made her lose control. But all that matters is that you're safe and you're here. We have a lot to prepare for.'

'Prepare?' My mind was sluggish again.

'Indeed,' my grandfather said, 'we will discuss it after the meal, when we are alone.'

Apparently 'alone' meant everyone save Dylan remained. He didn't complain though and wandered off, tempted by the lure of a great library, seemingly he had forgotten his wish to return to the ground. Erik had been about to leave as well when I raised a hand to my grandfather's arm and whispered in his ear.

'The boy stays,' he declared, Erik beamed at me and walked importantly to my side.

'You know, I guessed that you were hiding something,' he said as we crossed a tightly woven bridge, 'but I never imagined you'd be the princess.'

'So you're not angry with me for not telling you the truth?' I asked hesitantly, feeling relieved as he shook his head. We didn't get to say much more, as we entered another room with a circular table in its centre. Something shifted from the other side of the table, and I noticed a woman, not much older than myself, move away from where she'd been leaning against the wall to stand at Rakael's side. Her black hair was pulled back and her green eyes looked me up and down, much like Rakael's had done.

'This is Jesse,' Rakael said as a means of introduction, and I inclined my head before looking down at the table. There was a large map on it, along with little diagrams and arrows and miniscule words scratched under the names of towns. I recognised the outlines of not only the Eastern Lands and Scardia, but also the three realms of Karshka, Velkra and Felshkar. This plan seemed to stretch across our entire world, and I gazed down at the map, for a moment uncertain about my role in this. Suddenly, inexplicably, I wished that Markus was here. I wanted to feel his arms around me and hear his voice reminding me that I made my own fate, and that I could be and do anything. My heart ached with longing, and I reached absentmindedly to touch the copper coin that had lain at my throat since he gave it to me. As if sensing the turn of my thoughts, my grandfather's hand firmly grasped my shoulder. My hand stilled on the coin and then let it go, returning to my side.

'You can do this, Nina,' he said, using my preferred name for the first time, 'you were born to rule over Scardia and that is what you shall do. You're not alone anymore.'

'No, you're not,' Erik piped up at my side, his eyes burning with excitement.

'He's right, Princess,' Rakael said grimly, her steely eyes meeting mine across the table. Her hands spread across the map as she leaned towards me, her fingers inches away from the capital of Scardia and the palace, where the Usurper reigned. 'It's not going to be easy, but we will stand behind you to free our country. Now, are you ready to take back your birthright?'

I took a deep, reassuring breath and nodded. The time of running, hiding in the shadows and abiding by my three rules had reached its end. It was now time to reclaim my crown and free my country from the Usurper's reign.

Rakael smiled, her scar twisting across her cheek.

'Good,' she said, 'then let's get to work.'

Acknowledgements

There is the expression, "It takes a village to raise a child", and it is similar with writing and publishing a book – it is created thanks to many different people who have all had an input in this process. Firstly, I would like to thank my parents, my mother especially for being the first person to read the initial draft and providing me with unbiased advice.

I would like to thank my partner Jordan, for his continued support and encouragement. He always helps me to see the silver lining in every dark cloud and is a constant calming presence in my often-hectic life.

Finally, I would like to thank all the staff at the Book Reality Experience, Leschenault Press, for their support and advice throughout this process. I have highly valued their advice, contributions and ideas with the editing and publishing components of this experience.

About the Author

A booklover from an early age, Rose began writing stories from the age of seven and this passion continued into a life-long dream of becoming a writer.

When she is not reading a new book, jotting down ideas in a notebook or pottering around in her veggie garden under her cats' supervision, she can be found either on the stage in her other passion – amateur theatre – or teaching English and French to high school students.